"I could hear the two of you whispering at the door.

"I will never get used to people whispering. Never. I don't care what they say about me. I can handle remarks about blindness, but I can't stand people who think they know what's best for me, whispering behind my back."

A.J. stared at him for a long minute as her empathy reached out to him.

"I promise never again to talk about you when you're not there." The last few words began to break up, and she hoped he didn't notice. He must not hear her cry.

Vince touched her cheek, felt the wetness there and moaned. "Ah, damn, I made you cry. Don't. Please, Amanda. I can't stand it if you cry."

"It wasn't you. I wouldn't have hurt you for the world, but I don't pity you. Not one iota." She wrapped her arms around his neck. "You were my good friend once. I need someone to lean on just a little while. Please? You're the strongest man I know."

Dear Reader,

It's another great month for Silhouette Intimate Moments! If you don't believe me, just take a look at our American Hero title, *Dragonslayer,* by Emilie Richards. This compelling and emotionally riveting tale could have been torn from today's headlines, with a minister hero whose church is in one of the inner city's worst neighborhoods and whose chosen flock includes the down and out of the world. In this place, where gang violence touches everyone's lives—and will continue to touch them throughout the book in ways you won't be able to predict—our hero meets a woman whose paradoxical innocence will force him to confront his own demons, his own inner emptiness, and once more embrace life—and love. *Dragonslayer* is a *tour de force,* not to be missed by any reader.

The rest of the month is terrific, too. Marilyn Pappano, Doreen Roberts, Marion Smith Collins, Beverly Barton and new author Leann Harris offer stories that range from "down-home" emotional to suspenseful and dramatic. You'll want to read them all.

And in months to come look for more irresistible reading from such favorite authors as Justine Davis, Linda Turner, Paula Detmer Riggs, *New York Times* bestsellers Heather Graham Pozzessere and Nora Roberts, and more—all coming your way from Silhouette Intimate Moments, where romantic excitement is always the rule.

Yours,

Leslie J. Wainger
Senior Editor and Editorial Coordinator

FIRE ON
THE MOUNTAIN

Marion
Smith Collins

Silhouette®

INTIMATE ❦ MOMENTS®

Published by Silhouette Books New York

America's Publisher of Contemporary Romance

SILHOUETTE BOOKS
300 East 42nd St., New York, N.Y. 10017

FIRE ON THE MOUNTAIN

Copyright © 1993 by Marion Smith Collins

ISBN: 0-373-07514-6

First Silhouette Books printing August 1993

Printed in the U.S.A.

Books by Marion Smith Collins

Silhouette Intimate Moments

Another Chance #179
Better Than Ever #252
Catch of the Day #320
Shared Ground #383
Baby Magic #452
Fire on the Mountain #514

Silhouette Romance

Home To Stay #773
Every Night at Eight #849

MARION SMITH COLLINS

has written nonfiction for years and is the author of several contemporary romances, as well as one book of general fiction.

She's a devoted traveler and has been to places as far-flung as Rome and Tahiti. Her favorite country for exploring, however, is the United States because, she says, it has everything.

In addition, she is a wife and the mother of two children. She has been a public-relations director, and her love of art inspired her to run a combination gallery and restaurant for several years.

She lives with her husband of thirty years in Georgia.

For their contribution to this book,
I would like to thank Dr. J. L. Rabb
and Dr. Larry Davis, and especially
thanks to Norris Curtis.

Prologue

The sun was a huge fiery orb that hung over the horizon like a threat. The squadron of F-16s was flying at an altitude of 2,000 feet and at speeds in excess of 350 knots. They carried a full component of armament.

That much he remembered.

The desert floor beneath them was a colorless blur. But no one was looking at the ground anyway. Their eyes were fixed on the instruments, instruments so sophisticated that the humans who watched them were almost immaterial. Almost. The instruments mapped the road to destruction with a minimum of human input.

Those things he knew.

Afterward was a blank, like a vast hole in the tarpaulin of his memory.

He could have speculated, because that particular sortie was one of many he had flown in the two weeks he'd been in the desert, with just enough time in be-

tween one debriefing and the next briefing to grab a
bite at the mess hall. Or to collapse for a couple of
hours in his bunk. Or to take a tepid, brackish shower.

No beer. No booze. No women. Just do your job.
Do it fast, do it right, so we can get the hell out of here
and go home.

How did people exist in that climate?

"Major? Is there anything else you remember?"

The voice of the crash investigator brought him
back to the present—back to sounds and smells that
were not commonplace in his life, but were nonetheless recognizable: a cheerful voice in the corridor outside his hospital room, dishes rattling, cool crisp
sheets, the not entirely unpleasant odor of antiseptic.

The voice also brought him back to the grim, the
ominous—the pain inside his head, pain often so
acute, so corrosive that he suspected his brain had de-
cayed inside his skull, back to the heavy plaster cast
that weighted his left arm and shoulder, and back to a
world that was black. Utterly, unremittingly black.

Back to the blessed oblivion provided by the nee-
dle.

Vince Thornborough could have speculated, but the
man didn't want speculation. He sighed and shifted his
head restlessly on the pillow. "Nothing. Sorry."

Chapter 1

A. J. Upton brought her low-slung car to a stop between the two posts that delineated the entrance to her father's property, curved her arms across the top of the steering wheel and leaned forward to peer into the stormy September night.

Her headlights cut two useless oblongs through the heavy rainfall, while the wipers struggled in vain to keep the windshield clear. Her objective was some distance ahead, a dark, two-story blur at the end of this miserable excuse for a driveway. The nicest thing one could say about the track in front of her was that it was straight. Someone, sometime in the far distant past, had dumped a load of gravel haphazardly into the ruts, but the stone had long since washed away, leaving deep, water-filled trenches.

Alone in the car, A.J. spoke aloud to her absent father. "If I scrape something vital on my undercarriage, I'm sending the bill to you."

She kept her foot on the brake a moment longer, still hesitant to approach the dark, unfamiliar cabin for some reason. It was almost midnight. The dashboard clock, always slow, read eleven-forty-five. A combination of annoying delays had kept her from leaving Atlanta at a decent hour. Then this storm had hit when she was an hour north of the city, hampering her even more.

She realized dolefully that if the rain had come just a few days earlier, it would have demolished one of her father's arguments for sending her here in the first place—that the lack of seasonal rainfall had made brushfires a genuine hazard. Instead of climbing steadily through the north Georgia mountains for three hours, she could have been lying on a warm beach somewhere, enjoying her first real vacation in a very long time.

But her father, General John Upton, U.S. Air Force, had argued that it was not only necessary, it was her duty to come. "To make amends for your unfortunate actions fourteen years ago," he'd added in his most intimidating military manner.

Suddenly a bolt of lightning illuminated the area around the cabin fully. A loud clap of thunder followed almost immediately. The afterimage was burned into her mind.

The cabin was just as her father had described it, a two-story log building, rustic but sturdy looking, a perfect place for a bachelor, which her father had been since her parents' divorce when she was ten. He used the cabin for hunting and fishing—and someday soon, he would retire here. It was man's kind of place, he'd explained.

She'd never before been invited.

There was no light, no vehicle in the carport, no sign of life at all. The place was deserted.

"He must have decided to leave," she muttered aloud, referring to her father's friend and protégé, Major Vince Thornborough, who was supposed to be using the cabin. Vince was the model of an ideal military man, a born leader and according to the general, the finest pilot he'd seen in his twenty-nine years in the Air Force. "I can't say I blame him. This whole scene is spooky."

An image of Vince as she remembered him rose in her mind. Laughing, challenging eyes the color of semisweet chocolate, thick dark hair, broad shoulders and rugged build, strong white teeth contrasting with his olive complexion, masculine, cocky, sexy as hell. And angry, she added conscientiously, really angry at her. Of course, that was a long time ago.

She'd spent the past few days reminding herself that coming here was the right thing, the humane thing for her to do as a physician. And also trying to convince herself that, as a grown woman and a professional, she had no reason to be nervous around the man. In reality, she dreaded this meeting as much as she had ever dreaded anything. After what she had done, fourteen years was nothing.

But she had also been filled with a sense of anticipation that wouldn't be denied. The closer she'd come to the mountain cabin, the faster her pulse had raced. Even now, at the thought of him, her heart took a little jump.

To see him again, after all these years . . . She'd had such a crush on him. She'd called it love. Later she realized she had been going through an extra potent episode of youthful insanity.

Whatever her emotions had been in the past, they were now beside the point. The perfect pilot seemed to have flown this particular coop.

A.J. shook her head in resignation. She'd made this trip—through the storm and over dangerously twisting mountain roads—for nothing. Vince was probably with friends, having a drink at the officers' club in Marietta this very minute. She wondered if she was relieved or disappointed to find that he wasn't there.

Her father had told her where the spare key was kept, so at least she wouldn't have to look for a motel tonight. In the morning she would head south. Her fingers tightened their grip on the steering wheel. She shifted her foot, touched the accelerator lightly, let her tires find the ruts and slowly edged the car forward.

A bump jarred her teeth. Irritation drew her brows together in a scowl but, so far, there were no unpleasant sounds from beneath the car.

The driveway was lined with tall pines. Though the undergrowth was spare, the tree trunks seemed to crowd in closely, as though eager to fill the remaining strip of open space. She could see no more than a few feet beyond the verge on either side and she felt as though she was moving through a dark, forbidding tunnel.

At last, the driveway ended in a small clearing. She pulled her car into the carport that was attached to the cabin. She switched off the engine and sighed her relief that the trip was over. She sat there, relaxing for a moment, flexing her stiff fingers. Her immediate priority now was a bed; she hoped the sheets weren't musty.

When she opened the car door, the pounding rain on the tin roof drowned out all other sound. She stepped from the car and put her foot down in a run-off, soaking her sneaker. "Damn."

Her suitcase was in the trunk. The rain, aided by a gust of wind, soaked the back of her shirt and jeans when she retrieved the case. "You owe me, General," she said under her breath.

The cabin lock was stiff and she had to rattle the key before she could get it to turn, but at last the door swung inward. She gave a sigh of relief and felt around on the wall for a light switch.

Suddenly, without any warning at all, a figure from the darkness grabbed her wrist and yanked her over the threshold. Her shriek of alarm was instantly cut off. Her attacker had one of her arms behind her in a hammerlock and was choking her with his other arm. The next thing she knew, she was on the floor.

It all happened so quickly that for a second A.J. was too stunned to feel fear or fight back. But then she got one hand free. She twisted beneath him—it had to be a man, and a big one at that—raked her nails over a patch of skin and screamed bloody murder. She aimed a kick at his crotch but the angle was wrong and she kicked his knee instead. She heard his growled curse, then she was flipped over again; this time there was a knee in her back.

A.J. was small, only five-two, but strong. After several years working at a hospital in the roughest part of the inner city, she considered herself street tough. But she couldn't counter the strength of this man. She turned her head and rested her cheek on the cold floor, panting loudly. She tried to remind herself that panic was as self-defeating here as it was in the emergency room.

He hadn't really hurt her. Nevertheless, he was definitely in control of the situation. And this wasn't the city, where if she could get free and run fast enough, she could find a cop somewhere. On the way to the isolated cabin, she had passed no lights along the road, not for miles. For the first time, A.J. began to feel a frisson of fear.

"Who the hell are you and what are you doing breaking in here?" The man's words were low and gritty, delivered like rapid shots in the dark.

A moment of heavy silence followed his challenge, allowing her to identify a voice that she would never forget. Unbelievable. "Vince? What the hell are *you* doing?" she shrieked. "Get your knee out of my back. It's me—I mean, A.J.—John's daughter."

His grip eased slightly. *"Amanda?"* His tone was disbelieving.

Amanda. She closed her eyes on the memory. He was the only one who'd ever called her by her given name.

He turned her over and yanked her to her feet. His hands left her shoulders to cup her face, roamed quite freely over her breasts, the curve of her waist, her hips. It was done quickly, impersonally—for purposes of identification only—but his exploration left her warm with chagrin.

Abruptly, she found herself free. Her eyes had adjusted to the darkness and she could see his shape, no longer menacing. She could also hear him breathing hard. Subduing her had taken some effort, then. She smiled to herself. Good.

"Why are you sneaking in here in the middle of the night? Have you ever heard of knocking?" Vince demanded. But he was also calling up a mental image. Amanda Jane Upton! Good God, he hadn't seen her in—what was it?—twelve, fourteen years. By this time she must be a grown wo—

A sharp, unpleasant memory sliced into his thoughts and tightened his lips. He folded his arms across his chest. Hell! If he had his way, he wouldn't see the little troublemaker again for at least that long. What was she doing here? Especially now.

John had sent her, damn him. Why couldn't they just leave him the hell alone? The black world Vince lived in was heavy trouble at any time. Now he felt the weight of his anger increase like a burden.

"I didn't sneak," A.J. snapped in response to Vince's demand. She chafed her wrist and flexed her elbow to be certain it was working properly. Dislodged strands of hair hung in her eyes; she blew them away. "For your information, I found the key and unlocked the door." Now that her sense of danger was over, she was recovering her irritation—at him, at her father, at herself. The loose strands of hair fell into her face again. Angrily she jammed them into the twist at the back of her head. "When I drove up it didn't look like anybody was here. There was no car in the carport, and the house was pitch-black. Why don't you turn on a light, for heaven's sake?"

She realized her mistake immediately and touched her fingers to her mouth, but of course it was too late to recall the words. Dear God, of *all* the clumsy, thoughtless things to say.

When it came out of the darkness, Vince's laugh was low and bitter. "Why waste electricity?" he asked scornfully. "I don't know whether the light is on or off. And a car wouldn't do me a whole lot of good, now, would it? Besides, it's a little late for casual visitors."

"I'm sorry, Vince. I'm really sorry," she apologized. "That was a dreadful, insensitive thing to say. I wasn't thinking." She put out her hand to search along the wall for a light switch.

But he was there first; her fingers brushed his. She snatched her hand away as the light came on. They were in a small entry room, standing face-to-face, much closer than she'd realized. She backed up a step and was barely able to control her gasp of dismay.

Vince had apparently reached for the first item of clothing he came across, which happened to be a pair of cutoff jeans. They were partially zipped, but the top button was open, revealing enough skin and dark hair to make her certain that he was naked underneath. His near-nudity raised her temperature a notch, but that wasn't what had caused her to gasp.

His buddies called him "Ironman." It had been his handle fourteen years ago, and he was still called by that name.

But the strong, athletic man she had known was now haggard and gaunt. Above his waist she could see the clear outline of his ribs. His chest was still wide but the musculature there had lost some of its depth. His square, stubble-rough jaw was still firm and tenacious, but the skin above it was an ashen color. He seemed to have lost not only weight, but substance.

His shoulder bore the marks of surgery, now well healed. Another, deeper scar breached the hairline just above his temple on the right side of his head. She smoothed her palms down the legs of her jeans. Dear God, with an injury like that, he was lucky to be alive.

And his eyes . . . his beautiful dark brown eyes with their thick black lashes, were expressionless, empty.

Blind.

His F-16 had crashed in a Middle Eastern desert. He'd had to eject. Something had gone terribly wrong with the ejection mechanism, and he'd been knocked unconscious. He'd wandered, alone and dazed, in the desert for many hours, and when they finally found him . . . She squeezed her eyes shut, recalling her father's sorrow when he'd described Vince's ordeal.

"The doctors say that he could regain his sight someday," John said. "Both his optic nerve, and the brain tissue surrounding it, are seriously swollen and bruised. They can't make a conscientious diagnosis, though, until all the swelling disappears. And that could take months, maybe even years."

A.J. forced herself to study Vince more carefully, this time through her physician eyes. Allowing for the passage of years, she'd expected changes, and they were there.

"You haven't answered me. What are you doing here?" Vince demanded again, a combativeness in his tone that pleased her. He was annoyed, but there was no self-pity in his manner.

You always were quick. It won't take you long to figure it out.

"Amanda?" He touched his forearm, drawing her gaze to the angry red marks she'd made with her nails.

The sight added to her guilt. "I'm sorry I scratched you. I'll put something on it," she offered.

"I can take care of it myself. Talk." A roll of thunder punctuated his words.

"I'd be happy to explain it all to you, Vince, but could we close the door first? I know we need the rain, but I've been driving through this storm for a while, and I'd like to leave it outside." A chilling gust of wind came through the door to punctuate her words.

When he didn't answer immediately, she went on. "Please, Vince. I'm soaked, and I'm cold."

His expression didn't change. "That's your problem," he said shortly.

She made an effort to keep her temper under control and to sound reasonably pleasant when she spoke. "Look, it's late. I'm sorry I woke you. If you'd like to go back to bed, I'm sure I can find my way to an empty bedroom. We can talk in the morning."

"Not a chance. I'll show you where you can change your clothes into something dry."

Well, thanks a whole heap. Her sympathy faded. She put her hands on her hips, prepared to tell this jerk that this was *her* father's cabin; she had just as much right to be here as he did.

"Then I want to hear an explanation," he went on before she could form the appropriate words of rebuke. "Come on." He turned away from her, reaching for the edge of a utility table. But, she noticed, he used the table merely for acclimatization. He dropped his hand and led the way unswervingly into a darkened hallway.

"I'll just get my suitcase," she said to the empty door.

She grumbled under her breath, but she hastily retrieved her purse and her suitcase, which she'd dropped on the step, set it all inside and closed the door. She relaxed for a second, her sigh mournful. What a mess this was turning out to be. Not a fortuitous beginning certainly.

The room she was in had been adapted for her father's purposes. Lockers of the type she'd used in high school lined one wall. Fishing gear hung from coat hooks near a deep stainless-steel sink with a wide drainboard. Another drain was centered in the tiled floor. This was probably where they cleaned the fish— and whatever else. Everything was as spotless as an operating room. And as cold.

She shivered as she picked up her purse and suitcase again and followed the direction Vince had taken. The hallway was dark, but he had turned on lamps in a room beyond to guide her. When she entered, she saw that it was a den, or a great room of sorts, and quite large. The feeling of spaciousness was heightened by a vaulted ceiling.

She'd always been curious about this place. Now her interest got the better of her as she looked around. A side wall was dominated by a large rock fireplace. She glanced back the way she had come, acclimatizing herself; she was on the opposite side of the house from the carport. The far end of the room was glass, slippery mirrored panes that probably looked onto a spectacular view of the lake and the mountains when it wasn't raining.

"This is really nice," she said. After the driveway, she'd expected the cabin itself to be more rustic, if not downright shabby. But this room had a certain restrained elegance that amazed her.

"This way," Vince said. He was halfway up an open flight of steps on the remaining wall. "I'm in the first bedroom on the right at the top of the stairs. There are two others, both with their own bathrooms. Take your pick while I get a shirt."

A.J. followed him. She chose the room farthest from the one he'd disappeared into. She dropped on one knee beside her suitcase and flipped the catches. A dark red turtleneck of soft cotton knit was folded on top. She gratefully stripped off the wet one she was wearing, tossed it toward a chair and pulled the dry shirt over her head. Her jeans weren't as wet as she'd thought but she took the time to change them anyway, along with her wet sneakers. She brushed her hair out and restored the twist. At last she could postpone the meeting no longer.

She stood hesitating on the stairway. Vince had entered the room below from a set of double doors set in another wall. Her heart took a leap at the sight of him. This could develop into a distressing habit, she thought.

He'd put on deck shoes and a wrinkled blue dress shirt, sleeves rolled back and tails hanging free. He'd abandoned the cutoffs for a freshly laundered pair of jeans. His hair had been combed and he wore a pair of dark, aviator-style glasses.

The tinted lenses effectively hid his expression, but not his rigidly determined jaw. She sighed, mentally comparing him to her father.

Both men were determined, dogmatic and assertive. Both men liked to give orders, and both gave them effectively.

Vince clearly intended to hear her story right now. As she watched, he moved without apparent effort to the open side of a built-in bar and touched a switch. The glass shelves behind him came to life, revealing barware of every shape and size in addition to quite a liquor supply.

Well-stocked ceiling-high bookshelves, a desk, a mahogany card table and chairs cushioned in leather, a large-screened television and a stereo were all in this one room. The furniture was as she would have expected—large and masculine, practical, in easy-care colors—tones of forest green, saffron and terra-cotta, as well as easy-care materials—tables of oak, sturdy and strong, brass lamps, soft leather upholstery. A few natural-colored, woven rugs were scattered about on the hardwood floors.

"Would you like a drink?" asked Vince when she approached the bar.

She rested her elbows on the rich teak surface of the bar, her chin in her hands, and her toe on the heavy brass rail bolted to the floor. Nothing so ordinary as a bar stool, here. Real men drank standing up.

"Bourbon, Scotch, gin, vodka?" Vince went on, touching each bottle, correctly identifying them as he recited the names.

She was impressed, but she had no desire for liquor. A drink right now would simply increase her exhaustion. "I don't suppose you have any coffee?" she said.

"As a matter of fact, I plugged in the pot to reheat what was left from supper. If you don't mind warmed-over coffee, it should be ready."

"I'll get it," she said quickly when he would have moved. "Is this the kitchen over here?" She walked toward the double doors from which he'd entered moments before.

"Yes," said Vince after a brief pause. "You haven't been to the cabin before?" He followed her progress by the sound of her footsteps—louder on the hard-wood floors, muffled as she crossed the rugs.

"No, I've never—" She broke off. It probably wasn't a good idea to tell him that her father had never invited her. She paused at the door, found another light switch. "May I pour you a cup?"

His mouth tightened in response to the question. "Thanks, I can get my own." His voice came from right behind her. "I don't need a sitter."

"I didn't mean to imply that you did," she answered in equally terse tones as she searched the cabinets. She finally found a collection of sturdy mugs and took one down. "I was simply trying to be polite." She filled the mug from the old-fashioned percolator. The coffee looked like sludge, but drinking sludge was nothing new for her. It reminded her of the coffee in the doctors' lounge.

"Be polite to someone who needs it," Vince snapped. He felt a sharp pain behind his right temple and almost groaned aloud. *Not now!* "I have an aversion to people waiting on me."

"Good for you," she said as she left the room.

When Amanda spoke, he had to tamp down an unconscious twitch in his memory. Even when she was a teenager, the effect of her husky voice on him had always been like an itch that needed to be scratched. She had what was commonly called a "whiskey voice," a sexy, feminine alto that was slightly rough at the edges. When she spoke, it vibrated through his pulse like a tuning fork. With the added depth of maturity, her voice was deeper, even more stimulating and sensual.

Sensual? Good God, where had that thought come from?

He didn't *need* this, he thought desperately. He braced himself on the counter with his left arm straight and rubbed the area around the scar with his fingers as though he could massage away the increasing pain.

He'd lived in the darkness for a lifetime, it seemed. The doctors told him to have patience—they were ninety-five percent sure he would regain his sight. But often in the cheerless hours of the night, when he awoke to blackness, he questioned their evaluation.

Then he felt guilty—guilty because of others, men and women who didn't have his chance to see again, who didn't have a hope to cling to, who would always live in blackness. Or guilty because of colleagues and allies who had lost their lives. He was lucky.

Ninety-five percent lucky.

He'd gone through the classic period of grief, of feeling he'd lost a part of himself. He'd also suffered a memory loss, magnifying the feeling. He remembered nothing after his plane lifted off the runway at the base in the Middle Eastern desert.

He'd become accustomed to the blindness, as accustomed as one could ever be. He was coping adequately; he could take care of himself. And if the worst happened, if he fell into the five percent margin of er-

ror—well, he wouldn't think about that unless it was
a certainty. He sure as hell wouldn't borrow trouble.

The last thing he needed right now, however, was a
spoiled, bitchy woman like Amanda Upton coming in
here to—to—to do whatever the hell she was here to
do. He poured his own coffee and returned to the main
room.

She was sitting on the sofa. He hesitated. He didn't
know how he knew where she was, but he did. He took
a chair as far from her as he could get.

The last time he'd seen Amanda Upton, fourteen
years ago, she had been a tempting sixteen-year-old,
far too young for him to take a serious interest in.
Now, however, his remaining senses were telling him
quite plainly that she was very much a woman.

During the short fracas at the back door, he had
been made unquestionably aware that her promising
sixteen-year-old body had now ripened to lush curves.
Her scent was unusual. He couldn't quite place it—he
was dumbfounded that he even remembered—but the
scent, something fresh and yet spicy, was unique to
her.

Nonetheless, he resented her presence. Whenever he
thought of Amanda Upton, he thought of lies. He
took a swig of the hot coffee. "Your father's had this
cabin for quite a while. I've been here a few times. I'm
surprised you haven't. Don't you live in Atlanta?"

"I did until yesterday."

He waited for her to continue. When she spoke
again, her voice was light, amused. "As a matter of
fact, I've never been invited to come. John bought the
cabin as a retreat, where he and his buddies can hunt

and fish. I think he felt that a feminine presence would defile the place."

He heard the layer of antagonism that ran beneath the veneer of amusement. Anyone else might have missed the darker emotion, but he'd found without the sense of sight, his other senses were more acute. Besides, he knew them both.

So, she and her father had never reconciled their conflicts. For both their sakes, he was sorry to know that. He had met Amanda in Hawaii during his first tour of duty with the air force.

Her parents were divorced, and she had come for her annual summer visit with her father, John Upton, his commanding officer at the time. She was fourteen, a skinny little runt with braces on her teeth.

He had run into them a couple of times at the O Club. He had realized almost immediately that her relationship with John was not a close one. John treated her more like a guest he barely knew than a daughter, as though he wasn't quite sure what to do with her. And the youngster so obviously worshiped her father that it was almost painful to watch.

Vince was right out of flight training, a hotshot pilot, full of himself. But for some reason, when he learned she played tennis, he'd asked her to play a game. He wasn't sure why; it wasn't in character for him to spend time with kids. But he had made an effort to be kind to the teenage girl. His tour in Hawaii had lasted for three years. He continued to befriend her when she visited each year.

Until that last summer, until she had betrayed him.

He wrenched his thoughts away from that issue. "But you're here now," he said, waiting for an explanation.

"There's a good reason," she said hastily, too hastily.

"I'm sure there is," he acknowledged wryly.

"It's not what you think."

"And how would you know what I think if your father hadn't sent you here to check up on me?" he countered smoothly.

A.J. bit her lip, preferring the whole truth, but she'd promised her father that she would be vague when questioned. Clearly, John had expected him to deliver the third degree. "I can understand your thinking that way, Vince," she said. "But the fact is, I've recently quit my job and I'm looking for something in this area. John offered to let me stay here while I'm interviewing."

"Convenient timing."

"Yes, from your point of view, I can see how you would think so. And I'm grateful for a few days off, but I can't go without a paycheck forever."

Vince rested his head against the back of the chair and rubbed his hand over his jaw.

When he didn't comment, A.J. sipped at her coffee quietly and thoughtfully. Weeks ago she had begun to recognize the signs of burnout in herself. It was familiar because so many of her friends had been through it before her, some with devastating effects. Atlanta's largest inner-city hospital was understaffed and overcrowded, and after several years in the emergency room there, she needed a change. She'd decided to get out, to make the change herself before a decision was forced upon her.

She loved her profession; she wouldn't want to do anything else. But occasionally, over the past few, very difficult weeks, she wished she had a switch and could just turn off being a doctor for a while.

She submitted her resignation and prescribed a vacation for herself. Afterward, she planned to practice in a small, quiet town in the mountains of north Georgia. She was leaving the city for good. Let someone else suture the knife wounds, dig for the bullets, sweat out the drug overdoses. Let someone else comfort the children.

When her father had learned of her plans, he had faced her with his customary air of command. She remembered the conversation vividly. "Excellent. You can stay at my cabin while you look for a job. Take your time to find exactly the right place."

The unplanned burst of generosity was very unlike him. She was pleased. "Why, John—" She broke off, remembering that someone else was presently staying at John's cabin. "No, I don't think so."

"You're moving to the mountains? You're looking for a place to settle? Isn't that what you said?"

She'd tried to protest. "Yes, but—"

"Then the timing is ideal."

A.J. had sighed and tried again. "You of all people should realize that Vince will resent me being there. Get someone else to share the cabin with him."

Her father was quiet for a minute. When he spoke again, his voice was restrained. "There is no one else, A.J. He's in a volatile mood. You're the only one who could do this without question. You're my daughter.

It's my cabin. You're looking for a job in the area."
He spread his hands. "It's logical that you would
make the cabin your base of operations."

She'd rolled her eyes at the military jargon.

Her father went on without noticing. "Vince has
fired the housekeeper I arranged for, and he insists on
staying up there alone. With all the dry weather we've
had this summer, there have been a number of minor
fires in the area, and the cabin is isolated. The local
sheriff says it's possibly arson. I don't like the situation, A.J. I don't like it at all."

She focused on the first part of his statement, concerned despite herself. "Vince is alone? How does he
manage?"

"The state rehabilitation people helped set things up
for his convenience when he first got to the cabin. A
retired schoolteacher lives just up the road. He pays
her to come by every day. She shops for him, reads the
mail, things like that. And Ed Wilson is stationed at
Dobbins in Marietta," he said, mentioning the large
air force base in a suburb north of Atlanta. "You remember Ed? He and Vince were both in my command in Hawaii, and they were in the desert together.
He goes up every week or two."

A.J. had been relieved that her father hadn't waited
for an answer to his question about knowing Ed Wilson. She did indeed know the other pilot, and she did
not care for him. "Vince is not stupid, John," she'd
told her father, reaching for any and every excuse. "If
I show up there, he'll know you sent me."

"He may suspect, but he won't be able to kick you
out of your own father's cabin." He hesitated. "A.J.,
he's blind," he said with a rare trace of emotion. "Can

you imagine what that does to a man like him? On top of that, he has no memory of the crack-up. No one thinks he's guilty of mishandling the mission, but he's not cleared in his own mind. And won't be until he can remember everything that happened."

"Were there no witnesses?"

"None."

A.J. wished she'd been five minutes later entering her apartment; she would have missed John's call. She mentally thumbed through one idea after another, seeking an argument that her father would listen to.

"John," she said finally, "I am the last person in the world Vince Thornborough would want dropping in on him during his recuperation. He hates me."

He gave a snort. "That old business? He's forgotten that by now. What's it been, ten years? You were a child. Ancient history."

She felt the stain of embarrassment color her cheeks. "It's been fourteen years. And I guarantee you, he hasn't forgotten."

"Forgiven, then."

"I doubt that, as well."

"A.J., listen to me." John's voice again took on the tone of command. "If you insist upon raising that old issue, then think about this. You put Vince's career in jeopardy and made his life extremely uncomfortable for a while. I know you were just a kid, but it was your lie that got him into trouble, with me as his commanding officer, and with the air force. You owe him."

A.J. had had no comeback for that argument. Slowly, she'd nodded. She'd been a teenager, an adolescent in the very worst meaning of the word. Wild and careless. Never mind that she'd been competing for her father's attention. To her shame, she had almost ruined Vince Thornborough's future as an officer. Her father was right; she owed Vince. But could she face him, even after fourteen years?

"You are a doctor, A.J. Doesn't the Hippocratic oath say something about the obligation of doctors to help where they can?"

"Something like that," she had finally agreed.

Another roll of thunder over the cabin, and Vince's voice brought A.J. back to the present.

"Your excuse for being here is a very good one, Amanda," he said at last. "I would probably believe it, except that John has been scheming to get someone in here ever since I fired the housekeeper."

"I'm sure he's concerned," she offered, constrained to keep all emotion from her voice. "He's always thought of you as the son he didn't have."

He nodded, acknowledging the fact that both of them knew it. "I can't imagine that you came willingly, did you?"

Despite the perfect opening, he didn't mention the incident years ago, the conflict that still lay between them. She debated, then decided nothing would be gained by denying the truth any longer. Still, she didn't want to wrangle tonight. She was simply too tired to cope with a full-fledged argument. "I didn't come willingly, Vince, because I knew you would resent my being here. But it wasn't blackmail." *Not exactly.*

"I really am changing jobs, and I want to live in this area. I plan to arrange appointments in several small towns nearby. The cabin is conveniently located for my interviews.'' She set her coffee aside, rose and walked to the huge window beside the fireplace.

From her father's description she knew the cabin sat on a promontory with water on two sides. Tonight, however, the lake was invisible through the darkness and rain. Instead, the lit room behind her and the man she had come to see were reflected in the heavy glass.

Vince's expression was troubled. And she saw something else—pain, awful pain. As she watched, he put his fingers to his temple and rubbed in a circular motion.

She spoke quickly. ''I'll be away a lot. Some will be day trips and occasionally I'll be gone overnight. The cabin seems to be large enough for both of us to be comfortable without stepping on each other when I am here.''

''I don't think any place is that large,'' he murmured almost to himself.

Vince was grateful that Amanda had no comeback for his testy remark. He was tired, and clearly The Headache was going to stick around with him tonight. He'd learned to live with it, as though it were another creature—a monster—who shared the cabin occasionally. He walked the floors with it.

But he'd rather live with The Headache than with Amanda Jane Upton. What was he going to do? Hell, he couldn't deal with more than one monster at a time. He closed his eyes and massaged the back of his neck.

He turned back to her. ''I'd like for you to leave, Amanda.'' He didn't state the obvious, that it would be easier for her to go than for him. ''Not tonight. But tomorrow morning.''

A.J. waited for the other shoe to drop—but still he didn't bring up the ancient discord between them. She kneaded her eyes with her fingers. She tried to inject some lightness into her tone. "Look, Vince, I realize you don't like me very much," she began.

He muttered something under his breath that sounded like "Damned straight."

She chose to ignore the comment. "But could we finish this debate tomorrow? It's nearly 1:00 a.m. I've had a long day, and I'm really beat."

He wouldn't care that she had spent last night, Saturday, on duty in the emergency room. Or that she'd missed lunch and dinner and been caught in a formidable storm. Or that she'd had an awful drive through the mountains when she'd really wanted to go to the beach. He wouldn't give a damn about any of those things. She'd have to come up with a solid argument, and tonight she was simply too tired to think of one.

She waited—it seemed forever—until at last he moved, heading for the stairs. On the way he picked up his mug from the table, not faltering or hesitating. When he was halfway to the second floor, he paused and she held her breath.

"Unplug the coffeepot before you come up."

Chapter 2

A bright bar of sunlight struck A.J.'s eyes. She propped on her elbows and squinted, looking around, unsure at first where she was.

When she remembered, she collapsed with a groan, turning her back on the sunshine. This was the first day in years that she hadn't had to be anywhere.

The feeling was a little unsettling.

She thought of her life as a blur of constant movement, interspersed with brief episodes of total collapse. The last three years had been hell. At some point she would have to pull out the memories and deal with them. But not now. Now was the time for rest and healing and appreciation of a less stress-filled life. All she needed was time. She had a few doubts as to how easily she would adjust to small-town living. But she looked forward to trying.

She'd barely glanced at the room last night before falling into bed, but now she looked around and decided it was plain but comfortable. Serviceable. No frills. It was furnished with a maple bed with a matching bedside table, a chest of drawers and mirror and an upholstered chair with another table and lamp beside it. In the opposite wall was the door to the bathroom.

A.J. turned onto her back again. To her right was the uncurtained window. To her, a city dweller, a bare window was a menace that left her feeling exposed and unprotected. She supposed people felt differently in the country. However, if she stayed beyond today, she would find a quick solution to that particular problem.

Though Vince hadn't welcomed her with open arms, he hadn't thrown her out, either. Considering that she had lied about him, gotten him into deep trouble with his friend and commanding officer, she could have expected worse.

She stretched her feet under the covers, extending and curling her toes as she pictured the strangely vulnerable Vince. Oh, he hid it well. He'd become proficient, capable of caring for himself, but he was vulnerable to the handicap. There were things he couldn't do, would never be able to do if he didn't regain his sight. He couldn't fly, and he couldn't drive.

She smiled to herself, remembering how much Vince loved his cars. The same passion for speed that had led him to become a fighter pilot had led him to fast cars, as well. He would love hers.

Would he see again? She resolved to call his doctor to find out the full extent of his injuries and the latest diagnosis. Her father had said the military specialists were still optimistic that he would regain his sight.

But the doctors were military, too. They would know what Vince wanted to hear; they would hold out hope as long as it was possible to do so. She wondered what an honest evaluation would reveal.

She linked her fingers behind her head and stared at the ceiling. He needed to exercise and eat right. The hour or so she'd spent with him last night wasn't enough time to do any kind of thorough evaluation of her own. But from the way her father had described Vince's attitude toward his accident, she wouldn't be at all surprised to find that he'd dismissed the doctors' recommendations as easily as he'd dismissed the housekeeper.

Well, she would see to it that there were some changes around here. Her father was right. She did owe Vince something, and helping him regain his strength and vitality would go toward repaying that debt. She didn't even think about leaving.

She glanced at the clock. Seven-thirty. She rolled out of bed and headed for the shower. A short time later, dressed in jeans and a salmon cotton sweater, she twisted her hair up out of her way and left the room.

When she reached the foot of the stairs, the smell of coffee led her through the big room and to a door leading to a wide screened porch. The porch ran the length of the cabin across the back and overlooked the lake. She stepped onto a slate floor and looked around her with a smile of pleasure.

The rain had washed the air clean and, though the weather was cool and crisp, the bite of autumn was not yet uncomfortable. Every house she'd ever been in had a gathering place and she could tell immediately that, at least in good weather, the porch was the gathering place in this one.

Fixed as it was on the sunny south side of the cabin, it was warm and bright. A dozen sturdy wooden rocking chairs with cane bottoms were arranged in a long row overlooking the lake. In addition to the door to the main room, which she had come through, the porch also opened into the kitchen. A trestle table and chairs sat nearby. But the most surprising thing about the porch was the fireplace, a twin to the one inside with the addition of a large grill-like apparatus. The percolator was bubbling away on a thick wooden chopping block attached to the grill.

Vince sat in one of the rockers, staring out over the lake. A blue jay squawked from the branch of a tree outside, and he turned his head toward the sound but his expression remained unchanged. Her smile faded.

Vince Thornborough was as cool a customer as he'd ever been.

He was dressed in black jeans and a dark knit polo shirt. One ankle rested on the other knee and he moved the chair slightly with his foot. His mood seemed casual, easy, but she sensed that it was also resolute. She recalled his declaration last night that he didn't need a sitter and wouldn't have anyone wait on him. Clearly he was going to renew his demand that she leave.

A.J. was certain that the radio playing softly in the background masked her footsteps. Nevertheless when she stepped through the door his head swiveled in her direction. She stopped, self-conscious that she'd been caught staring at him.

Remembering suddenly that he couldn't know she was staring, she caught her lower lip between her teeth and closed her eyes briefly. At one time she would have reveled in the opportunity to look at her hero to her heart's content. Now she could only strive to control the compassion she felt, lest he hear it in her voice and take it for pity.

"Coffee smells good," she said lightly as she headed toward him.

The tinted glasses were in place. She knew that there was more than a cosmetic purpose for his wearing them. In his condition, the pupils continued to absorb light, but their normal reflexive action, contracting and expanding to guard against damaging the retinas, was inhibited.

"It's almost ready," he told her, rising. He headed toward the kitchen. "I'll get the mugs."

She started to offer to help, then bit back the words. No point in annoying him first thing in the morning. She started toward a chair, but instead of sitting down she detoured to the edge of the porch, looked out over the lake to the mountains beyond. "I like this porch," she said, loudly enough for him to hear.

He answered from the kitchen. "John added it after he bought the cabin."

The lake was not a large one, probably no more than ten or twelve acres, but, set as it was in a beautiful hollow of fir trees and hardwoods and surrounded by mountains, it was like a small jewel. No breeze ruffled the placid surface. A reflection of blue skies, fluffy white clouds and a small thicket on the opposite bank was as clear as a photograph.

A family of Canada geese seemed to have made a home in one section of the shore where the undergrowth had not been cleared. Squirrels scampered up and down the tree trunks near the cabin, busily scavenging and storing the last few available nuts before cold weather arrived.

"Here we go," said Vince, startling her. He set the tray he was carrying on the chopping block and picked up the percolator.

She hadn't even heard his approach. His talent for knowing where she was standing was a bit eerie. "Thank you." She took the mug he'd filled. "This place is really impressive. The lake is so smooth, you'd never know it stormed last night."

"Have a muffin," he said, ignoring the comment.

"You cook, too?" she asked, picking up a napkin from the tray. She didn't inquire about the third mug on the tray. "Are these blueberry muffins?"

"Mountain blueberries. But the bakery did the cooking. I can manage to feed myself. I don't starve. But I don't try anything fancy."

She took a bite of a warm muffin, her mind storing that gratifying piece of information. "Mmm. They taste like homemade."

Vince set his coffee on the table beside his chair and headed for the far end of the porch. Just then the sound of a car's engine reached her ears. "Company?" she asked.

He kept walking. "A neighbor who picks up my mail. She comes by every day."

This must be the neighbor her father had told her about. "You must have ears like a bat. I didn't hear a thing."

He didn't answer, just moved the broad shoulders in a gesture of dismissal. His indifferent attitude this morning was a bad omen for her plans.

A woman entered through a screened door, her slender face and ear-length bob the perfect complements to her neat figure. She was pretty in a grandmotherly way, having made no compromises with her age. Her makeup was light. She was dressed neatly in stylish slacks and a sweater, but her hair was unapologetically gray.

"Good morning, May," said Vince. "You're early."

May held several envelopes and a colorful newsprint flyer. "The mail was early this morning," she said cheerfully as she riffled through the batch. "You got an advertisement for the sale at K mart, Ed McMahon wants to give you ten million dollars, the electric bill came and—ah, here's one that seems promising. Smell."

As he obediently inhaled, his expression softened. A hint of a smile played at the corner of his mouth.

A.J. was surprised at the sudden change in him. It was the first sign of softening she'd seen since she arrived. He was fond of the woman and clearly they'd played this game before.

"Mmm, lilacs. Let me see, that would be either Jannine in Malibu or Diana in Virginia Beach."

May crowed with laughter. "Wrong. It's your credit-card bill. They must be having a perfume sa— oh dear." She broke off as she caught sight of A.J. "I didn't realize you had company, Vince."

"Not company," he said shortly, the smile melting from his face. May came quickly toward where A.J.

was sitting. "May, this is Amanda Jane Upton. She's—"

"John's daughter." May took A.J.'s outstretched hand as she finished his sentence for him. "Of course," she said kindly. "I'm May Cameron, and I'm so happy to meet you at last. I've often heard John speak of you."

A.J. was surprised by both the statement and by the woman's warm greeting. "How do you do?" she said as her hand was grasped.

"Fine, thank you. I'm so glad John convinced you to come," May went on. She settled in the rocker next to A.J. and smiled affectionately at Vince when he handed her the third mug. "Thank you, dear. A.J., this stubborn man has the misguided idea that he is completely self-sufficient. He does extremely well, but he really shouldn't be living alone."

A.J. felt her heart sink. May had known in advance of her arrival, but Vince had not. It wasn't like John to be careless. Or was his carelessness deliberate?

Vince had returned to his chair. She glanced at him, assessing his reaction to the woman's comments. His face, what she could see above and below the dark glasses, had grown tense; his mouth was a hard, thin line and his brow was forbiddingly furrowed.

May didn't seem to notice that anything was amiss. "I guess you won't need me anymore, Vince, now that A.J. is here."

"A.J. is looking for a job in this area. She will be away interviewing some of the time," he said harshly. "Our agreement still stands."

Even May, cheerfully determined as she was, couldn't ignore the chill in his voice. It seemed to disconcert her. "I'm sorry, Vince. I thought..." She trailed off. "Of course, I'll be glad to keep to our— Do you need anything from town today?"

He didn't have to intimidate the poor woman, thought A.J. She opened her mouth, but before she could form the words of protest, he spoke.

"No, not today," Vince said more gently. "And the bills can wait a day or two. But I would like to drive into town with you sometime this week." His annoyance having eased, he finger-combed his long hair and gave a rueful grin. "I think I need to go to the barbershop. What do you think?"

May looked from Vince to A.J.

A.J. raised her brows and shook her head. She was no more going to offer to drive him to town than she was going to explain her father's rudeness.

"I think you certainly do," May agreed. The leading question had permitted her to recover her cheerful demeanor. "Do you want to go this afternoon?"

"A few more days won't matter," he said.

A short silence followed while they all sipped the hot coffee. The radio continued to play softly. May was trying to catch A.J.'s eye. But A.J. wasn't about to start playing a silent game of Twenty Questions. Vince was far too adept at knowing what was going on around him.

"Have you heard the news this morning?" May asked at last, breaking the silence.

"Yes, I heard a report a few minutes ago," said Vince. "The story was sketchy, but I gathered there was another fire late yesterday afternoon," he added.

"On High Top Mountain," confirmed May. "It was small, like the others. The sheriff thinks this one was malicious mischief, too, like the others. It was probably set deliberately by foolish kids showing off."

Vince grunted.

"This is the third of these fires," May explained to A.J. "None of them has been large enough to be dangerous so far, but I don't mind admitting that I'm getting a bit nervous."

May went on. "They found several beer cans at the scene, just like before. The sheriff is going to the high school today to talk to the kids."

"Are there houses on High Top?" asked Vince.

"Just three, but the fire wasn't close to them. It was off one of the old logging roads. If the storm hadn't brought some rain last night, this one could have been worse than it was." She set down her cup and got to her feet. "Well, it's almost eight-thirty. I've promised to substitute at the elementary school for a few hours today. One of the teachers has to take her daughter to the dentist."

"May, if it's going to be inconvenient for you to stop by..." Vince began.

"It isn't inconvenient at all," she assured him with a pat on his arm. "Just let me know when you want to go to town."

"Thanks. I'll see you tomorrow." He left the two women and disappeared into the kitchen.

"I'll walk out with you," said A.J.

"I seem to have said the wrong thing," said May when they were outside.

A.J. wasn't surprised when the older woman raised the subject. "John should have warned you if he wanted Vince to think my being here was a coincidence.''

May gave a derisive snort. ''Your father called last week to say that you would be coming soon to stay at the cabin. I assumed he had told Vince. He didn't say a word to me about playing dumb.''

A.J. decided she liked this woman. ''My father's never been known for his subtlety. He's always expected people to know what he was thinking. He probably didn't think of explaining.'' She smiled and plunged her hands into her pockets. ''Where is this High Top Mountain you spoke of?''

May indicated the tallest of the series of peaks beyond the lake. ''The one next to that is Squirrel Mountain, then Low Top, then Runaround. We're on Snake River Mountain.'' She hesitated. ''He's very proud of you, you know.''

A.J. stopped dead in her tracks. ''Who?'' she asked blankly.

''John, of course.'' She shook her head somberly as she went on. ''He really has been worried about your working in such a dangerous part of the city. I'm sure he's pleased about your plans to move.''

May continued toward her car and didn't see A.J.'s reaction. Her father was proud of her? It was the first *she'd* heard about it.

''Well, I suppose I'd better continue to drop in each day,'' May said as she climbed into her car.

A.J. recovered quickly. ''Vince was right. I am going to be looking for a job in this area, and I may have to be gone overnight. He seems to be coping well, so it probably would be a good idea not to disrupt his schedule.''

She waved as May reversed and headed down the gravel track. Then she turned back to the house. So her father had told May that she was a doctor, a doctor that he was proud of, no less. Why hadn't he ever told her that? At one time his praise would have meant a lot.

She shrugged off her regret as she stepped over the threshold. She had other things to think about.

Last night with Vince she had avoided the subject of the kind of job she was seeking, but at some point May was sure to mention her profession. She would be smart to tell him before he found out by accident.

She stifled a groan as she thought of his probable reaction. He resented her being here in the first place; he would resent her even more if he thought there was a medical reason for her presence.

She didn't even consider lying to him. A lie had started the trouble between them years ago. If she was to be any help to him at all, she would have to be completely honest. She straightened her shoulders, determined to face him immediately.

Vince had disappeared. She assumed he was upstairs. She explored the bookshelves as she waited to see if he would return. She wanted to get this confrontation over with as soon as possible.

Finally, when he didn't reappear, she went looking for him. If his bedroom door was closed, she would forget her confession for now. But the door to the bedroom was ajar and she could see him sitting in a large easy chair with his feet propped up on an ottoman. He wore a headset of some kind; a cassette case was open on the table beside him. The dark glasses dangled from his fingers, and his eyes were closed.

She swallowed a lump in her throat as she looked at him. His legs were crossed at the ankle, his hands relaxed on the arms of the chair. His dark hair was rumpled; his pale features were slack, defenseless and infinitely sad. He would not want her—or anyone—to see him exposed and disarmed like this. She backed up a step.

Without warning he opened his dark brown eyes, pinning her with an angry scowl where she stood. She inhaled sharply, an apology on her lips.

Then she remembered that he could not see her, a fact that intensified the aura of vulnerability. She blinked against a sudden well of tears.

Without another sound, she backed away.

When Vince appeared a couple of hours later, A.J. was in the kitchen and the place was filled with enticing aromas. Shutters disguised an eating counter between the main room and the kitchen, and it was there that she'd arranged the meal.

"Hi," she said brightly when she saw him. "I'm fixing lunch. Have a seat at one of the counter stools."

"I don't eat lunch," he answered shortly. The glasses were back in place.

"Well, I hope you're going to eat this lunch. There's far too much for one person. Cream of mushroom soup—homemade, of course—spinach salad, cheese toast and my famous boiled custard."

He hesitated. "That's too much food for four people," he said, but he finally sat on the stool in front of the counter. "And you didn't find all that in the refrigerator."

"No, I made a quick trip to town." A.J. set a bowl of the steaming soup in front of him. "Soup's in the middle, salad at ten o'clock, iced tea at two."

His hands moved across the place setting. She would have sworn they didn't touch a thing, just hovered, but when he picked up the spoon and tasted the soup, there was no hesitation in his motion. "Soup's hot." He set down the spoon, picked up a fork and began on his salad. He took a couple of bites before he paused. "Aren't you eating?" he asked mildly.

"Yes, of course." She circled the counter and sat on the stool beside him. She picked up her own fork. They ate in silence for a few minutes. "Well, what do you think?" she asked finally.

"You're a good cook."

"Thank you." The edge was off her appetite, so she laid down her soup spoon. This was as good a time as any to get her revelations out of the way. She swiveled her stool toward him and said, "I was admiring your kitchen. You have everything set up efficiently. You said you cook for yourself?"

His mouth twisted. "I've had help from the rehabilitation people. And enough time to learn a few basics."

"I noticed the 'high marks' on the stove." The bright orange, raised dots were impossible to miss. They were painted on the oven regulator and the dials for the eyes of the stove in increments that were easily read with the fingers. On the microwave the numbers had been traced with the same orange marks.

"How do you know about 'high marks'?" he asked, setting down his spoon.

She didn't hesitate. "I'm a doctor, Vince. Didn't John tell you?"

When he spoke, it was in a soft tone of disbelief, and the awful hard look disappeared from his face. "A doctor? You?" He turned his stool until their knees were almost touching.

"Yes, me." She wished she sounded more confident but she was affected by their close proximity. She gazed up into his masculine features. Up close, his pallid skin tone seemed to have taken on a tinge more color than she'd thought earlier.

But his mouth had not changed. Not in all those years. She stared helplessly at his lips, at the study in contrasts there—hard and soft, firm and pliant. She would have given anything to feel that mouth on hers fourteen years ago. *What about now?* asked her inner voice.

Cut that out! she answered, and continued her visual exploration. The corners of his eyes bore a fan of squint lines. Pain had delved into the slash in his cheek and the lines bracketing his mouth, making them deeper. Dear heaven, he was good-looking, not classically so, but ruggedly, virilely handsome.

She felt warm, unsettled, deeply affected by his nearness. After all these years, she should be able to control her feelings. He was a friend; he needed help. She would concentrate on what she could do.

His incredulity didn't really surprise her, but she *was* surprised that it pricked her ego. When she spoke, her voice was subdued. "I've changed a lot since... since..." She trailed off.

"Since all those years ago when you made a fool of both of us?"

So, the incident had been on his mind. It had only been wishful thinking on her part to hope that maybe he'd forgiven her. She should have known better.

"No," she said after a moment's hush. "Since I made a fool of myself and got you in trouble." She swallowed the lump in her throat and went on in a quiet voice. "You thought John had blackmailed me into coming here. He didn't. Everything I told you was true. But he did have a strong argument. He said that I owed you mightily for what I did fourteen years ago."

The silence was so thick it would have absorbed a clash of cymbals. "Nonsense," he said briskly. "You don't owe me a thing."

"I'm not so sure." She thought she'd only mouthed the comeback but his hearing was acute.

"I told you, I don't need a sitter."

"Are you going to kick me out?" she asked, hoping he wouldn't hear the strain in her laughter.

"Of course not. If anything, *I* should go, but it would be damned inconvenient. However, this is your father's place. No one has a better right to be here than you."

She caught her breath. "That isn't true. John's a lot closer to you than he's ever been to me," she said softly.

"Oh, for God's sake," he said impatiently. "Let's not get started on your complaints against your father. I should think you'd have outgrown that."

Her chin came up. "I have," she stated bluntly. "My father's indifference is no longer important to me. Maybe we can work out something. A schedule maybe, that would keep us out of each other's way?"

His brow knitted in a frown but before he could speak she went on. "And—I—if it's possible, I'd like to clear the air of old hurts, Vince. I'd like to apologize for everything that happened fourteen years ago."

His expression was closed. "You were a kid, Amanda. This isn't necessary."

"It is for me." She rested her elbow on the counter and massaged her temple with two fingers. "I was reckless and headstrong that summer. I'd like to think I've changed."

"You must have," he said bluntly and without forgiveness. "I can't imagine you with the self-discipline to get through medical school."

"Neither could John. I had to come out of college with a 4.0 average for him to believe it." She smiled slightly, then the smile faded. "Knowing the politics of the military like I do, I'm sure there are still people who believe you were responsible for my escapade."

After a minute, he said in an even voice, "There are a few."

"I would be wary of those people, Vince. They obviously don't wish you well."

"But you do?"

"Yes, of course."

Vince made no further comment, but his mind was working rapidly as he turned back to the food. He would never forget that night. For once Sir Galahad hadn't ridden to the rescue. She'd ended up in jail—or juvenile detention—and he'd been blamed for her ordeal.

The kid was now a grown woman. A doctor.

He shook his head, unable to merge the two images. He found it impossible to imagine the Amanda he had known as a medical doctor. Without a doubt, that girl had been amply intelligent to study for a medical degree, but she had lacked the patience or the will.

But she'd had the fire and the passion, he remembered abruptly. How could he have forgotten? The whole time he'd known her, she'd been a passionate advocate for the causes she believed in. He recalled the earnest lectures he'd listened to on any number of topics—the environment, the dolphins, recycling.

He wondered if she ever unshackled that passion now—if she ever let go. As a kid, she was a delight to observe when she focused on an issue. The image was as clear in his mind as though he could see. Her deep blue eyes would be full of fire, her skin would glow, all her tremendous energy would coalesce on her subject.

Malarkey, he reproached himself. *You seem to be forgetting that the last year, the subject was you.* Amanda Upton was no longer a girl, he reminded himself again. As though he needed reminding.

The atmosphere was quiet, hushed, as they finished lunch, interrupted only by the clink of silverware and the hum of the refrigerator.

So, John had sent Amanda to the cabin deliberately. He'd suspected as much. And John had told May to expect her, but he'd neglected to warn Vince. Vince was fairly certain that his friend would have a great excuse for that particular lapse.

Suddenly Vince's hand, the one holding the spoon, halted in midair halfway to his mouth. He wondered what kind of doctor she was.

The spoon clattered as it hit his bowl. "Amanda, if you are a psychiatrist, I'm leaving, and to hell with what's practical," he said adamantly. He was through being anyone's guinea pig. He just wanted to be left alone to heal. When he'd regained his sight...then he would worry about his memory.

A.J. chuckled. "I swear to you I'm not a psychiatrist," she assured him. "I'm board-certified in emergency care."

Relieved, he returned to his soup. She really was a terrific cook. "What is board-certified?"

"I've passed some pretty stringent tests, and I've been working in the emergency room at City Hospital for the past three years."

"Good God." Vince scowled as he absorbed this information. The downtown hospital in Atlanta was the place for the victims of violence, the drug users, people who'd been shot or knifed, the highway accidents. "You must have had some ugly experiences."

A.J. laughed softly and without humor. "It was pretty grim at times." A few of the more depressing memories thrust themselves into her consciousness now, but she resolutely pushed them away. She wasn't ready to deal with them yet. She'd promised herself time and she was going to keep that promise. "But the work is rewarding. It moves fast, and it's vital."

"Why are you leaving City Hospital?"

"I want to settle down to a slower life-style, live in a smaller town."

He raised a brow at the idea. "You're awfully young to be talking about a slower life-style."

She was suddenly defensive. "Age doesn't have anything to do with the choice I've made. I'm not like you and my father, Vince. I have no desire to live my life on the edge.''

Vince wondered why, if her statement was true, she hadn't gone into dermatology, but he wisely didn't voice the thought. He recalled something she'd said a few minutes ago, almost as a throwaway remark, about John being closer to him than he was to her. "Do you and John get along now?"

She got up to serve their dessert. "I no longer blame him for my unhappiness, if that's what you mean."

"You had no reason to blame him, except that you were the product of divorce. Many kids go through that and survive."

"I wonder what kind of emotional baggage they take along, though." A.J. returned to the stool beside him, took a long breath and let it out. "I really don't want to talk about this anymore," she said as she began eating her custard. "I rarely see John these days, and that suits both of us."

A few moments passed before Vince said, "John has never been as bad as you painted him. You wanted to believe the worst."

The smooth, sweet taste of the custard turned sour in her mouth. "Believe it or not, Vince, I've grown up. The discipline of medical school has a way of encouraging maturity," she said with exasperation. "Are you finished with your dessert?"

He nodded.

She scooted their plates through the opening so she could reach them from the kitchen side of the passthrough. "Once I faced the fact that I was unimportant to him, he became unimportant in my life, too.

Now we can be friendly when we see each other, and that's enough.''

"Is it?"

"Would you like anything else to eat?'' she asked, a signal that, as far as she was concerned, this conversation was over.

After a minute he shook his head. "No, thanks. I enjoyed the meal.''

"I'm glad,'' she said in automatic response. "I enjoy cooking. So, is it okay with you if I stay here?''

"I've already told you, it's your father's cabin.''

"But—''

"Damn it, Amanda,'' he erupted. "I can't very well throw you out, now, can I? Drop the subject!''

The telephone rang into the silence that followed his outburst, startling her. "Shall I answer?'' she asked, looking around. There was a phone on a table next to the sofa.

But Vince had already reached through the opening and grabbed the wall-mounted unit in the kitchen. "Hello.'' He listened for a second. "Yes, just a minute.'' He held out the receiver to her.

A.J. took the phone, and he stalked away.

It was her mother calling from Florida, where she lived with her second husband and the twin boys of that marriage. It took A.J. a moment to switch from being the focus of Vince's anger to Jane's.

"Why didn't you tell me you were moving?'' Jane demanded without preamble. "I had to call John to find out where you were.''

Oh, dear, Jane wouldn't like having to do that. "I wrote to you and mailed the letter yesterday before I left Atlanta, Mother. But you knew I'd been planning this for a long time.'' She tried to inject a note of repentance to pacify her mother.

Jane was not mollified. ''We were expecting you to come here for a vacation before you moved. How long are you going to stay at your father's cabin, and who was the man that answered?''

''The man is a friend of John's. The cabin is quite large enough to accommodate more than one person. I told you all about it in my letter, Mother. You should have it tomorrow. Now, tell me, how are the boys? And how are you?''

Having the subject switched to herself always improved Jane Leander's temperament.

Chapter 3

Vince came inside from the porch and headed for the kitchen. He wasn't sure what he was going to do about Amanda. His first instinct last night had been to run like the devil was on his heels.

But where would he run to? He decided he'd better see if he could carry on a halfway cordial conversation with her. If not, he'd be on the phone to Ed Wilson this afternoon to come get him the hell out of here.

He heard the clink of dishes being scraped, and water running in the sink, smelled the sharp lemon scent of the detergent as Amanda filled the small cup in the dishwasher.

"You finished your call?"

"Yes, it was my mother calling from Florida," she answered unnecessarily.

He nodded. "I seem to remember you have half brothers, don't you? Twins?" he asked. "How old are they now?"

"They'll go to college next year."

He heard the softening tone and something else—pride?—in her voice as she went on. "They have already been scouted for tennis scholarships."

Vince knew that Amanda's mother was a tennis instructor who had given up a promising career as a pro when she'd married John. The loss of her dream had been another challenge to the marriage. "Does your mother still dream of training a champion?" he asked.

"Mother wasn't successful with me, but the boys seem to be producing for her."

"You sound like you're proud of them."

"I am. They're nice kids."

"So you've forgiven your mother for devoting so much time to her second family?"

She hesitated. "Yes," she said quietly.

And he knew he had her. He didn't even have to voice the obvious. Instead he said, "If you're going to cook, I'll clean up from now on," in an attempt to set up some kind of balance between them.

"I don't mind—"

"I'll clean up," he snapped.

"All right," A.J. answered.

He shoved his hands into his pockets. God, this situation was offensive to him. He hated to be beholden to anyone for anything. Since leaving the hospital, he had learned to take care of himself with a bare minimum of assistance.

The county rehabilitation people had come in to teach him the basics of getting along on his own and equip the cabin with the necessary contrivances, like the high marks on the stove. With their help he had rearranged the furniture in such a way that he wouldn't be constantly tripping over a table or running into a chair. They also provided the books on tape that had saved his sanity.

He'd faced the ominous fact that there would be some things that he couldn't do until he regained his sight, but for those things, May was the only outside help he needed. He paid her a comfortable amount to check in with him each day.

She read his mail and wrote the checks to take care of his bills. She shopped for him, arranged and labeled his food and his laundry. And, though he tried to schedule necessary trips, like those to the doctors in Atlanta, during visits from his friend Ed Wilson, occasionally May chauffeured him when he needed to go somewhere.

The arrangement suited them both. He felt that he was retaining a certain independence, and the money he paid May was a nice supplement to her retirement income. He didn't mind the compromise—it was better than the housekeeper who had constantly dogged his footsteps.

When he grew bored, Ed Wilson was always quick to answer an invitation. And John came to the cabin periodically. As long as they were both stationed nearby, he was in good shape. They were his friends, and he didn't mind asking for help or companionship.

But, for some reason, he hated like the very devil to be beholden to Amanda Upton.

"There's some of the soup left over. I'm putting it— let's see—on the second shelf of the refrigerator. It is still in the saucepan, so if you want some, all you have to do is reheat it."

"Thanks." Vince shoved his hands into his pockets and continued to lounge against the doorjamb. He seemed to be waiting. A.J. wished he would go away; he was making her self-conscious. She took her time, trying to ignore him as she finished rinsing the dishes, then stacked them in the dishwasher and wiped off the countertops. At last she dried her hands and turned to him. "Are you waiting for something, Vince?" she asked curtly.

"Yes," he said unexpectedly. "I'd like to braille your face."

"What?" If he'd asked her to strip, she couldn't have been more surprised. "Why?"

"I have a picture in my head that doesn't quite jibe with what you've been telling me. Of course, it's been fourteen years, but I'd like to judge for myself. At any rate, it's easier for a victim of blindness to 'see' the person he's with if he can touch them. Do you mind?"

Mind? Of course she minded. Having him in her space made her nervous. He was much too sharp. He might see things through his fingertips that she didn't want him to know. "I'm not sure."

"Come on, Amanda," he mocked in a wry tone. "You're not afraid, are you?"

"Certainly not," she responded, eyeing his relaxed pose against the door casing. His hands in his pockets tightened the faded jeans across his hard, flat stomach and outlined the generous contour of his sex. She *was* afraid, she admitted to herself. When Vince got close enough to touch her she felt a weakening response that was far too dangerous for her to deal with. *Right now,* she added to herself. *Only because I'm burned-out right now. In a week or two, when I've had a chance to...*

"Then sit on your stool."

She tossed away the towel she'd been holding and brushed past him. "All right."

As soon as she was seated, with her legs together, heels hooked over the foot support and her hands folded in her lap, he came to stand directly in front of her. Her knees were pressed against his flat belly.

His fingers brushed her forehead, skimmed lightly down her brows. The pads were slightly callused, and they set up a tingle as they moved across her features. She smiled. "That tickles."

He withdrew immediately.

"I wasn't complaining." She took his big, warm hands and returned them to her cheekbones, knowing despite her words that this whole thing was a mistake. He was too close. And his nearness was having the same effect on her as it had all those years ago. Which, of course, was ridiculous. She was no longer an impressionable girl. She was a woman now. There was no reason for this warm, soft feeling in her chest.

Although he couldn't see her, his face filled her vision. She used the moment to study him. His dark hair held no hint of gray, and she wasn't sure she agreed with him that he needed a haircut. It reached below his collar, but it was shiny clean and looked silky to the touch. She gripped her fingers together, deciding she liked it long and slightly disheveled.

Though she didn't have to guard her expression, she did have to strive to keep her breathing even and quiet. She wasn't completely certain she succeeded.

He was older but his youthful good looks had only improved with age. She wished again that he wouldn't wear the dark glasses. She desperately wanted to see his face unguarded. His mouth was as sensual as it had been at twenty-four but now the lines that bracketed it were deeper, a suggestion of the suffering he'd endured. The young man he had been was now submerged in the harsh experiences of a seasoned adult.

She wondered what his mouth would feel like on hers. The prospect was thrilling, almost as electrifying as the effect his moving fingers were having on her skin. Briefly she closed her eyes. Then she thought she felt a tremor through his fingertips.

When she opened her eyes again, she knew she was mistaken. A smile played around the corners of his mouth as he studied her. She wasn't sure what kind of smile it was, but it was not a smile of amusement. Nor was it one of pleasure.

He traced the shape of her nose and lingered on her lips, brushing his thumb back and forth across the lower one, setting up shivers along her spine. He tracked the line of her chin, then he returned to her cheeks, her ears, stroking the shell-like curves, fingering her lobes, before moving across her head.

Her hair was gathered at the back of her head into a severe chignon, the way she always wore it. He hesitated, his hands cupping each side of her head. His palms were warm, comforting; the tingling warmth within her had become an undeniable flutter. He was so tall.

If she leaned forward, as she was tempted to do, she could rest her face against his chest. Even her nape, where a few baby-fine curls had pulled out of the hairstyle, didn't escape his exploration.

The scar at his temple drew her gaze. It disappeared back under his hair and she wondered how far. Without thinking, she raised her hand to touch it.

Instantly he dropped his hands and stepped back, just one step—but at the separation she felt chilled, as though they had been cleaved by an icy partition.

His expression was hard and serious, and he stood for a moment, defensively. "Ugly, isn't it?"

She barely noticed the strain in his voice. She was breathless, winded as though she'd been running, and still doing her damnedest to conceal it from him. "Ugly? No." She looked again. "The erythema has almost completely resolved," she said absently.

He frowned. Folding his arms across his chest, he dipped his chin as though he were looking down at her. "The what?"

She smiled. "Sorry. The redness has almost completely faded."

"Good." He paused but the frown remained on his face. "Why do you wear your hair in that severe style, Amanda?"

The question surprised her. "Because it's easier. And it looks more professional that way."

The noise he made might have been a laugh or a rebuff.

"It's true." She chuckled. "You probably don't remember how curly it is. When I was in medical school, I tried wearing it short. It was easier to keep, but all those curls around my face made me look like I was four years old. Patients find it difficult to trust a youthful doctor. A short, youthful doctor."

He nodded, keeping his expression noncommittal. "I guess I can understand that. Is your hair still the same color?"

She put her hand to her chignon and frowned slightly. Why all this interest in her hair? "It's still dark. I never got the nerve to go blond."

"How tall are you?"

"You would ask me that," she said with a wry smile. "What did you used to call me? The runt. Well, I'm still five foot two, still a runt. I haven't grown since I was sixteen."

He digested that information for a second. "If I remember correctly, I changed that nickname to 'Tiger' after I saw you on the tennis court. You never married?"

She shook her head, then realized he couldn't see her. "Nope," she said in what she hoped was a nonchalant tone. "I've come close once or twice, but I can't seem to find the right person. Anyone who would put up with my hours is either a hypochondriac or another doctor. I would have nothing in common with a hypochondriac and *too* much in common with another doctor. How about you?" she asked, though she knew the answer perfectly well.

He combed his fingers through his hair. It settled back into place. "No."

Something about his answer, some tension in his voice, as though he might say more, made her glance at him. But his dark eyes were still hidden. She had never realized how difficult it was to read the feelings behind another person's words if you couldn't see their eyes. And she'd never realized that without observing those feelings, you couldn't really understand what they were saying.

Deep thoughts, A.J. Too deep. She hopped down from the stool. The atmosphere between them being fairly friendly at the moment, she decided to gamble. "Let's go for a walk around the lake."

"No, thanks."

"Why not? It's a beautiful day. It would be good for you—fresh air, sunshine, all that nice stuff."

"I said no," he said more firmly. "I'll be upstairs." He turned away.

She supposed she should be grateful—the past few minutes he'd been almost friendly. But as a doctor she wasn't going to let him get away with this. "Are you going to have a workout on the weight-lifting equipment I saw in your room upstairs?" she asked, watching his back. The equipment was one of the one-piece designs that took up very little space. It worked on the principle of tension to give a workout that was as effective as old-fashioned weights and barbells. "I've seen good results in some of my patients who used that same piece of equipment." She was careful to keep her tone positive because the equipment in Vince's room looked brand-new, as though it had just been taken out of the box.

He slowed his steps but he didn't answer.

"Do you need some help setting the tension?"

"No, thanks."

"Oh? Had you rather sit in your chair with a headset on and feel sorry for yourself?" she went on. "Come on, Vince, if you don't want to work out, at least walk around the lake."

Finally he turned on her, an angry look about him. "Do you think I'm going to shuffle around that lake, clinging to you like a life preserver?" he snarled. "I'd just as soon be in the cockpit of a plane. The rehab people set the tension on that damned weight machine."

She was taken aback by his outburst and reminded of something else she missed about Vince. She missed the swagger, the hip-rolling, self-confident stride that was a part of him. And it saddened her even more to realize that he, too, was aware of its loss. "I think you're a bit of a coward, Vince Thornborough," she accused softly. "You have to get on with your life."

His back stiffened. She could clearly see that he wanted to protest, to defend himself.

Come on, she urged silently. *Blow up, get mad, do something!*

"Think what you want. I don't care," he said heavily. Then he continued toward the stairs without looking back and without saying another word.

A.J. sighed. She shouldn't have made the accusation, not even in a teasing tone. But seeing him like this depressed her greatly. She grieved for him and couldn't control the urge to do something.

She forced her memory back fourteen years, searching for a clue that might suggest a solution. It was like taking a patient's case history, she told herself. Except in this case she knew very little recent history. She would have to poke around a little bit, try to get him to open up or talk to her father. In the meantime, she could use the knowledge she did have. Some things, some characteristics, about a person didn't change.

What characteristics had marked Vince Thornborough, had been peculiarly his?

He was honorable, patriotic, kind to children, old ladies and pets.

No, no. She needed more than that. More personal things.

Okay. He was always impatient and restless if forced to be inactive for a long period. She remembered that. He hated to have to wait for a tennis court. That one had possibilities.

And he always had an opinion, a comeback, for any remark, whether it was a joke or a serious comment. He never let her have the last word. He seemed to have abandoned that one, she thought wryly, recalling his parting remark.

She would continue to try to light a fire in him, to wake him up. She would goad and prod until she got a response. It went against her grain to see such a vital and dynamic man surrender to a solitary existence as Vince had done. She began to plan—and first on her agenda was another trip to town. She'd seen a sign this morning advertising the very thing she wanted.

"Hello, I'm back," A.J. shouted from the back door. She dropped her packages on the kitchen counter then returned to her car for the last of her purchases.

The dog wriggled and squirmed in her arms. She'd talked to him all the way back from town to the cabin, explaining what she wanted him to do. Every time she glanced over to make sure he was paying attention, he'd risen on his hind legs, with his paws on her arm, and licked her cheek.

He was perfect, she thought with a grin—three-quarters golden retriever according to the lady at the animal shelter. And he was blessed with the breed's characteristically intelligent eyes.

She had planned on a smaller dog, a beagle maybe, but this one was destined to be hers, especially when she heard that he'd been there for a month and they wouldn't be able to keep him much longer.

He was a very smart dog, the young woman had assured her. "He's almost purebred, you can see that. He'll be great with children," she'd said after A.J. had paid the fees.

A.J. had smiled to herself. She just hoped the dog was good with adults, terminally stubborn adults like Vince Thornborough. He needed a dog, she thought. She wondered why the doctors hadn't recommended he have one. Not necessarily a Seeing Eye dog, but a companion dog. One who would bark when a stranger approached. One who could walk in the woods with him. A dog to talk to, to touch.

And this dog was adorable, she added to herself as she set him down on the kitchen floor. He explored the area, which didn't take long, and headed for the great room. It took him a little longer to investigate the perimeter of that room, wagging his tail all the while, but presently he stood at the foot of the staircase and looked back over his shoulder at her, as though asking permission to proceed.

She nodded, smiled in anticipation and followed as he headed up the stairs. She heard one sharp joyful bark and saw his tail quicken before he disappeared into Vince's bedroom.

Then, "What the—get off of me. Amanda!" he yelled. "What the hell's going on? A.J.!"

She reached the door to see Vince struggling under the weight of the dog, who had jumped onto Vince's lap and was licking his face.

"Oh, I'm so sorry," she said, not sorry at all, of course.

"Where did this dog come from?" growled Vince, who was trying to evade the lapping tongue. He had been listening to his headset and now it was draped around his neck and the dog was chewing on the cord.

A.J. entered the room and took hold of the dog by the stomach, trying to tug him off of Vince. "Oh, dear, down, boy. I wanted to introduce you properly. This is my new dog."

She knew she was chattering but she feared she would burst out laughing if she didn't keep her mouth busy. The dog was doing exactly as she had instructed—smart dog—and now he wanted to stay where he was. "Come on, puppy. Come on," she urged.

"Puppy?" snarled Vince. "Good God. He must weigh twenty pounds."

"He is heavy—he's part golden retriever, and they get quite large. He isn't a puppy," she admitted, "but he isn't grown, either. The man at the pound said he was probably about six months old."

Vince finally managed to dispose of the animal by simply getting to his feet.

The bewildered dog landed on his belly with his paws going in four different directions. Finally he managed to right himself.

"Get him out of here," Vince ordered.

When A.J. didn't immediately comply, he added, "Now!"

"All right, all right," she said. "Come on, doggy. Come with A.J. I'll give you a treat."

The dog sat down at Vince's heels and looked up at her as though to ask, "Did I do right?" His tongue lolled out of his mouth. She would have sworn he was grinning at her.

She smiled back, then she tugged at his ruff but he refused to move. "I bought a collar and a leash. I'll have to get them."

"Hurry up."

She flew down the stairs and was back in a minute. "Here we go. Nice doggy."

The dog was perfectly willing to wear the bright red collar but he took exception to the leash. He slithered between Vince's legs and threatened to unbalance him.

"Sit!" said Vince.

Recognizing the voice of command, the dog sat.

A.J. snapped the leash on. "Thanks," she told Vince. "I'm sure he'll mind better when he gets accustomed to me."

His expression was forbidding. "A.J., I know what you're doing, and it won't work. I don't want a dog."

"*You* don't?" She pretended surprise to cover up her dismay at what he'd called her. This was the second time he'd called her by her initials. "I don't know what you're talking about, Vince. This is my dog. I've wanted one for ages but my condominium wouldn't allow pets. I'd made up my mind the first thing I was going to do when I got out of the city was to buy a dog."

He looked directly at her. She would swear he could see, so intent was his stare. Finally he spoke. "Just don't forget, he belongs to you."

She dragged the unwilling dog outside. He immediately perked up when he saw all the trees.

"You didn't do too badly," she told him. "It's only a matter of time. No one can resist a loving dog." I hope, she added to herself. He ran around her legs, pinning her with his leash. She laughed.

Vince sat in the easy chair, headset dangling from his fingers, and listened to the sounds the pair of them made from outside his window. Though he couldn't understand the words, he could hear the amusement as she talked and scolded and laughed.

The sound of her laughter, like her voice, had always had an effect on him. It was low and musical, and he'd never been able to hear it without smiling himself.

Her face. The sensation of warm skin under his fingers had been unfamiliar. It had been a long time since he'd touched a woman at all, and even longer since he'd been truly curious about one.

Her forehead was smooth, the brows arched; the eyes were slightly tilted as he remembered them being. Her cheekbones were high and well-defined, her nose was straight and her ears were small. But her hair, scraped back like that, was an offense.

He remembered her hair as a thick, glorious fall. Coffee colored. Beautiful and free. She wore it in a clasp when she played tennis but the rest of the time it swung past her shoulders, moving, shining with life and good health.

Her lips were still full and firm—as was her chin, he added, the last thought filling him with a feeling of satisfaction. She'd always been determined, and he'd admired her for it. He remembered the sweat he'd had to work up to beat the tiny slip of a girl on the tennis courts. He'd really liked her, liked her guts, her vivacious smile.

She hadn't grown taller, she said. So the top of her head should reach to a point just short of his chin. He rubbed his palm along the arm of the chair, wondering what her body was like.

That last summer in Hawaii, when he didn't like her at all, when she even didn't like herself . . . he'd been stunned when he saw her at the beach. He remembered the temptation of her uptilted breasts, her firm shapely bottom, the shameless bikini. . . .

Suddenly he felt an unexpected itch of desire.

He immediately put the headset on and punched the Play button. But he had difficulty picking up the thread of the plot of the latest bestseller.

Amanda was grown now, a successful professional. He'd been celibate since the crash—and not by design. He was bound to be physically aware of her.

But he would never forget what she had done to him years ago.

She'd thought herself in love; he knew that and he'd tried to be gentle with her. But that summer, her adolescent crush had become far too intense. To complicate the matter, she was also jealous because she thought her father was closer to Vince than he was to her, his own daughter. Those two emotional situations had produced weeks of turmoil. Eventually her lie had nearly cost him his career.

But all that was in the past. Another unrelated thought occurred to him. John would retire next year. If Amanda was going to live nearby, father and daughter should bury those long-standing resentments. This was an opportunity for them to have the close relationship that they'd never shared before.

He wondered idly if there was something he could do to help heal the breach between father and daughter. He thought a lot of John and knew the older man was dreading retirement.

Aw, hell. Why bother? Their relationship was none of his business.

A.J. wandered along the edge of the lake with the dog. Sand had been brought in at one time, and there was a small stretch of beach. A fresh breeze swept the water, producing miniature waves along the shore.

Vince had only called her A.J. one other time since she'd known him: the last summer in Hawaii, the last time she'd seen him. Even her memories were embarrassing, and she set them aside for a moment while she pondered his reaction to the dog.

She'd never minded her nickname but had always cherished that one intimacy Vince allowed himself. Last night, her unexpected arrival had to have disconcerted him, but he'd called her Amanda. When she'd informed him that she planned to stay, he'd still called her Amanda. When she'd admitted that she was a doctor and that her father had wanted her to check on him, he'd clung to the old name. But meeting with the dog seemed to have been the last straw.

What did you expect? She'd vowed to herself that she would prod him into anger and action. His resentment toward her would be a natural result.

She sat down, slipped off her sneakers and socks, and buried her toes in the cool sand. Thoughtfully, she watched the golden retriever play in the shallow water.

She closed her eyes and let the breeze cool her face. The memories would no longer be denied. Vince's use of her nickname had brought all the humiliation, all the difficulties of that last summer to the surface, forcing her to examine them.

A.J. had just turned sixteen when she had gone for her annual visit with her father, again in Hawaii. She could hardly wait to get there. Things at home in Florida weren't so hot. Her mother and stepfather were absorbed with her twin half brothers. But that didn't stop them from overruling her choice of friends, coming down hard on her for the least violation of curfew and generally screwing up her social life.

She arrived to find that John was nearing the end of his three-year tour of duty and was deep into readying the organization for its incoming commander. Like her mother, he had little time to spend with his teenage daughter. She felt like a wishbone, pulled apart by unfulfilled longings. She wanted to belong completely to one of them; instead, each gave her just a little time, just a bit of attention, enough so that they could deny neglecting her, not enough for her to feel secure in the love of either of them.

At least her father let her have some freedom. Just as she had for the past two summers, she played a lot of tennis with Vince Thornborough. That made up for everything.

Two years before, as an awkward fourteen-year-old, A.J. had developed a crush on him. He had always been indulgent. From the first, he seemed to recognize her loneliness. And she knew he genuinely enjoyed their tennis games because they were well matched. Both of them were intensely competitive and while he, of course, was stronger, she made up for that lack with swiftness, hustle and a streak of pure feminine guile, which seemed to amuse him. But that year, when she'd returned as a reckless sixteen-year-old, she realized she was wildly in love.

Vince absorbed her thoughts when she was awake and her dreams when she slept. Her emotions were in a perpetual turmoil, with the intensity that only the young can feel. She desperately wanted his attention, and she went about getting it in the most offensive ways. She made up flimsy excuses to be where he was; she was impertinent in front of his dates; she talked too loudly, drove too recklessly, stayed out too late.

After the first few weeks, she realized that Vince was making a distinct effort to distance himself from her. He had broken several tennis dates when she finally, boldly confronted him about his neglect.

Later, she would admit to herself that he tried to be kind, to let her down with as much grace as possible. But she pushed. At last, she got a grim and very unpleasant lecture on appropriate behavior for underage girls and was told she was not only a spoiled brat but also a pain in the ass.

She was angry, furious at him, then horribly embarrassed and properly humbled. She decided finally that she would be glad when this trip was over and she could return to her mother's home in Florida. She would even be glad to see her stepfather and the twin half brothers who usually drove her up the wall. She avoided Vince Thornborough and her great love shriveled like an old apple core.

She now pulled her knees up to her chest and wrapped her arms around them, trying to contain her misery in the curve of her body as the other memories rushed in.

Suddenly a wet tongue licked her cheek, rousing her from her reverie. She looked around, at the lake's gentle surface, at the sturdy cabin. She listened to the wind's soft sigh through the pine branches and sighed herself. Later. She would think about that later.

She wrapped her arms around the dog's neck and buried her face in his ruff.

She'd made an awful mistake, but she'd paid for it. She'd lost the friendship of a wonderful man. And she'd fractured her halting communications with her father, leaving damage that had taken years to repair.

She felt a weight of sadness on her chest and, determinedly, she cast it aside. "That was then. This is now," she said to herself.

That evening, A.J. sat at the large desk in the main room of the cabin, writing letters to the public hospitals in the area. The dog was resting his head on her sneaker-clad foot, but he immediately abandoned her when Vince walked through to the kitchen.

"I thought I'd have a glass of milk and snack before I go to bed. Can I get you something?"

"I'd love a glass of milk. How did you know I was here?" she asked curiously.

"Your perfume," he answered. "And the dog."

I'm not wearing any perfume, she started to say, but the words died on her lips. He had reached down absently to scratch the dog behind the ears. Her smile was one of satisfaction.

"What are you doing?" he asked.

She looked down at the papers before her as though she didn't know herself. "Oh. I have a list from the physicians' placement service. I'm writing to the hospitals in the area that interest me."

He nodded and continued along his route with the dog trailing along behind him. She heard him go to the cabinet, then the refrigerator. He didn't fumble or hesitate. He was back in moments and handed her a glass. But instead of leaving, he took a chair near the desk and rested his ankle on the opposite knee. He took a large bite of the sandwich he'd made.

"I smell peanut butter," she said, tapping her pen against the desk.

He finished the bite and swallowed. She was distracted by the play of hard muscle in his square jaw. Every inch of this man shouted "male." "Want one?" he asked, holding up the sandwich.

"No, thanks." She reached for the glass of milk and took a swallow.

"Which are the hospitals that interest you?"

She raised her brows over the rim of her glass. A friendly overture? She gave a wry chuckle. "My list has broadened considerably. It seems that quite a few hospitals in the area are looking for emergency room doctors."

He drained his glass of milk. "I'll leave you to finish, then. You'll lock up?"

"Sure. Good night, Vince."

The dog rose to follow.

"Stay," said Vince.

The dog looked to her for guidance, cocking his beautiful golden head to one side. His tongue lolled, and his pretty brown eyes were knowing. She shrugged.

She worked for another hour, then let the dog have a brief run outside before locking the doors and turning out the lights.

And so ends the first full day, A.J. said to herself as she climbed the stairs. All in all it hadn't gone too badly. He seemed to have accepted her presence—and the presence of the dog. With a certain reluctance, she amended, as she passed his door. He was on his guard about the dog, and her profession, and her cooking. Other than that, all had gone well.

At least they weren't snarling at each other as they had been last night at this time.

The dust blew in swirling eddies, clogging his throat, his eyes, his nose. He couldn't breathe as he staggered through the desert. But he had to find the place he was seeking. It was around here somewhere. He knew he was close, but the damn sand kept him from getting his bearings. He could have been walking in circles—*was* walking in circles, he confirmed, when suddenly he was in the air above the scene. Through breaks in the sand cloud below him, he could see the tracing of his own footprints, round and round in a blurred circle, leading nowhere.

Now he was falling back down into that blinding hell, falling quickly. He braced himself for a bone-jarring impact. But instead of the ground, a huge yawning hole appeared. He continued to fall, down, down into the darkness that had no bottom. . . .

Vince awoke, sweating profusely, the sheets in a tangle under him. He sat up on the side of the bed and wiped his face with both hands, not surprised to find that his hands were shaking badly.

He went into the bathroom and splashed cold water on his face and chest. His breathing slowed, as he felt for a towel and dried himself. With a last sigh, he opened the medicine cabinet and felt for the aspirin bottle.

Suddenly he had a mental picture of the weight-training equipment that sat in the corner of the bedroom. His hand fell, empty, to his side.

After a minute, he tossed the towel around his neck and, holding both ends in clenched fists, went to stand in front of the apparatus. He closed his eyes and stood there for a long time.

Slowly he extended his hand to feel the polished metal surface. It was cool. . . .

Chapter 4

A.J. and Vince were finishing lunch one day in the middle of the week. "If you like, I could drive you into town for your haircut," she offered, firing the first salvo in her battle to get him moving and out of the house. Her frustration was mounting, but she dreaded the impending encounter.

The first few days she'd spent at the cabin had gone fairly well. But she had to admit that the reason was Vince's rock-bound determination to avoid her. She cooked, and he seemed to enjoy the food. They ate together, and he was courteous. He always cleaned up the kitchen afterward. Other than mealtimes they rarely saw each other. The atmosphere remained cordial only as long as she didn't push him.

The situation frustrated the devil out of her. She hated waste of any kind. As a doctor, she was accustomed to people reacting positively when she offered her help.

She would like to intercept the mail and stop the delivery of those damned tapes. He had gone as far as letting the dog in his room during the day when he was listening to them. But he also used them as the most efficient way to shut himself off from the world.

He needed time to grow accustomed to having another person in the house, she rationalized. So she'd given him time, several days.

A stranger to idleness, A.J. had spent those days reading, and walking or jogging on the path around the lake and trying to contain her restlessness. One morning she had gone into town with May and had met several friends of the older woman.

It had been a pleasant experience, and clearly she had needed a few of those. She had needed the calm, quiet hours of relaxation. But no more.

Now she waited impatiently for him to answer.

"No, thanks," Vince answered after a long pause. He wondered why he refused at all. He needed a haircut.

But his antipathy toward accepting help from Amanda grew stronger each day. He had discovered, unexpectedly, that she was the last person he wanted to see him at a disadvantage. He knew that his attitude was pointless, even irrational. But no matter how many sermons he preached to himself, he still felt the same way.

She didn't argue with his refusal, or even answer at all. Which was odd, until he realized the silence was anticipatory. They were sitting in their usual spot for meals, side by side at the counter of the pass-through to the kitchen. She wanted to say something else—he could almost feel the vibration of her unspoken words. "Was there something else?" he asked, when she didn't speak.

Her tone was offhand. "Well, if you won't let me drive you to town—I'm not a barber, but I could probably trim your hair for you if you like."

At the idea of her standing body-to-body close to him, her hands combing through his hair, Vince's pulse took off like a rocket.

She'd been here for less than a week. It was no coincidence that he had stayed as far away from her as possible. The first day she was here, he'd realized that he was turned on by her—or, as he tried to convince himself, by his memories of her. He'd told himself that these unexpected feelings of desire were only brought on by his celibacy and the vivid images of her sexy little body as it had been at sixteen.

Back then he had felt guilty, though he'd only been twenty-four himself. But that kid was John's daughter. John, who had been like a second father to him, who had understood his love of flying as his own father, a farmer, never had.

There was a definite up side to his present feelings, however—the happy fact that his body was finally returning to normal thanks to John's daughter. He should be ecstatic and he was, in a way. The timing could be better, but he wasn't going to deny his relief.

A week or two after he'd been released from the hospital and had moved into the cabin, Ed Wilson had brought a couple of women friends up to spend the weekend. After his date had gotten over the initial awkwardness of his handicap, they'd had a pleasant time.

The woman had come to the cabin a few more times. She'd been amusing and playfully affectionate, and he'd enjoyed her company. But he'd been sexually indifferent.

Nothing there, he'd realized with consternation. He had absolutely no feelings of desire.

Not much got by Ed. His friend had teased him later—laughing and dramatically blowing taps in his fist for the stud of the squadron. Ed's jab had angered Vince at first. But then he'd shrugged it off.

The appellation itself was an exaggeration. Vince had never been a stud, which by his definition was a man who pursued women merely for the sake of conquest. He'd always liked women, genuinely liked them, their softness, their curves, their laughter, the way they smelled and looked and felt in his arms. He had enjoyed a healthy sex life since his college days. His sight was gone; was he going to lose the pleasure of physical intimacy, too?

He'd worried like hell until his next appointment with his doctors. They had reassured him that passion and desire would return just as his sight would— eventually. Their words had brought no comfort. He wasn't even sure he believed them. Until now.

The radio, tuned to a soft, sweet rhythm-and-blues station, played in the background. Amanda was waiting for him to answer. He tried to turn the subject of a haircut into a joke. "Does it look that bad?"

"As a matter of fact, no. I like it long. It makes you—" She broke off. "Never mind."

That she liked his hair long surprised him. "Come on," he said, crossing his arms on the counter of the pass-through. He followed her progress by sound. "You can't begin a statement like that and not finish."

"Yes, I can." She picked up their plates and headed for the kitchen.

"You shouldn't, then. Leave those dishes," he said. "You cook, I clean up."

She opened the dishwasher, turned on the water to rinse the dishes. Immediately she turned it off again when he came to stand beside her. His fingers circled her wrist and he took the plate out of her hand.

"Amanda, what were you going to say?" he repeated firmly.

He wasn't going to let her evade. After a minute she relented. "Long hair makes you look..." She paused until the atmosphere crackled with expectation. "...sexy." The word was blurted out.

Vince chuckled, hearing an unfamiliar self-consciousness in his own laugh. "Don't ever let the officer of the day hear you say that."

"I know. Maybe that's what I like about it. The unmilitariness." This time it was A.J. who gave a self-conscious laugh. "Is that a word?"

"Probably not," he answered. Together they resumed stacking the dishes, and neither of them spoke again until they had finished.

"I'm going to take the dog out for a walk," Amanda told him with a trace of restraint lingering in her voice.

He filled the detergent cup and pushed the button that started the dishwashing cycle. "I thought you were going to cut my hair," he said.

Then he wondered what in the world had possessed him. The risk was there—he'd admitted it to himself. Well, it was too late now to recall the words. He would just consider this a test of some kind.

"Okay. After I take the dog out."

He heard the door slam. While she was gone he roamed the room, pacing the familiar route he'd mapped out for himself. When he heard them returning a few minutes later he plunged his hands into the pockets of his jeans. "Where shall I sit?" he asked.

"I hadn't—I don't know," she said with satisfying confusion in her voice. "Think about it for a minute while I get a towel and scissors."

He could hear the click of the dog's nails on the bare floor as he followed her up the stairs.

Vince sat in the captain's chair in front of the desk. And waited.

A.J. found a comb and scissors, grabbed a towel from her bathroom and started back downstairs, wondering why in the world she had ever suggested cutting his hair. This was not the kind of event she'd intended when she'd determined earlier to goad him into action. She had neatly avoided close contact with him for several days; why mess up a good record?

Well, she had made the offer. There was no way she could get out of it now without seeming timid.

Vince had settled into the desk chair. She eyed him for a moment. "That chair puts your head a bit high for a runt like me to reach," she said, looking around. There was a short, armless, backless stool beside the bookshelves. She picked it up and brought it over. "Sit here, on this stool, instead."

She arranged the towel around his neck and took a deep but silent breath. The comb slipped through his shining hair. She made certain the part was straight, then she began to clip the hair on that side.

"You're cutting it pretty close, aren't you?" he quipped.

"Be quiet, Vince," she said, removing his tinted glasses and setting them on the desk. He immediately closed his eyes. "I have to concentrate. You don't want to lose a piece of your ear, do you?"

He chuckled. "I hope to hell you don't say things like that to your patients."

"My patients in the emergency room are usually unconscious. They rarely know whether I nick a body part or not." She paused to comb through the hair she had just cut. "That looks pretty good," she pronounced. "Sorry for the gallows humor. You tend to lose your sensitivity fast at City Hospital."

"I can't imagine you losing yours," he said, suddenly serious.

"Why do you think I left?"

He thought for a minute. "I think if you had actually lost it, you would still be there."

A.J. didn't reply, and he didn't speak again.

The dog watched while she worked in the back, trimming to just above his collar, and then she began to work her way around until she was standing in front of him. "Let me see if I got it even on both sides. Move, dog."

"I wish you'd give this animal a name." Vince snapped his fingers, and the dog came instantly to his other side. He scratched the silky ear. When he realized what he was doing he dropped his hand. "Sit," he ordered.

Until she was standing between Vince's legs, A.J. hadn't realized how tantalizing the position would be. She closed her eyes for a minute in an attempt to quiet her racing pulse. It didn't work. Heat from his large body surrounded her, warming her legs, her stomach, her breasts. Her body tingled with the beginnings of desire.

She opened her eyes, tipped his chin and took a step back, to judge her work from a safer perspective. It didn't work. The sound of her breathing, loud in her ears, was growing more and more shallow with her attempts at keeping it at a regular rhythm.

The offer to cut his hair had been a disastrous one, and she felt like a fool. Her objectivity, which she nurtured and cherished as a doctor, was shot to hell by his physical closeness.

Her instincts, equally valuable in her profession, told her that Vince Thornborough was an ongoing threat to her peace of mind. This had never happened to her before, not with someone she considered a convalescent. Of course, she'd never had a patient whom she'd once been crazy about, either.

She would not make such a mistake again, she promised herself. By disposition, she was a toucher. But it would be far more judicious for her to stay as far away from him as possible.

"That looks good," she said cheerfully, feeling better now that she'd made the vow. "Now I'll trim the front." Her thigh brushed the inside of his leg as she stepped forward again. She inhaled sharply. Or at least, she thought the gasp had come from her.

Vince clenched his fists to keep from reaching out to cradle her bottom in his hands. The sound of his breathing resonated in his head. He hoped she would think it was the dog panting.

He hoped she would finish quickly.

"Have you gotten any answers to the letters you sent?" Vince asked A.J. Friday afternoon. His question was delivered in a neutral voice. He stood at the back door, one hand holding the screen door ajar.

A.J. was on the ground beside the back stoop, feeding the dog, and she glanced up over her shoulder at him.

Her eyes narrowed. He seemed to be staring fixedly at her, his free hand shoved deep into the pocket of his jeans. He looked worried, his expression severely at odds with his casual question.

They had been exceptionally polite to each other, but their conversations had been kept to a minimum since the day she'd cut his hair. Now what was going on?

She wondered if he had sensed how affected she was that day. By the time she had brushed the hair off his neck and folded the towel, she had been trembling. She had given herself a lot of credit for not settling down on his lap and threading her fingers through that silky clean hair while she kissed him passionately.

She folded over the top of the bag of food and stood up, dusting her hands off on the seat of her jeans. "No, but I wouldn't have expected an answer this quickly. I only mailed them at the beginning of the week." She picked up the dog's water dish and crossed to the outside faucet. The autumn chill had finally taken hold in the mountains, so she wore an old windbreaker she'd found in one of the lockers. She had to push the sleeves up.

"Ed Wilson is coming tomorrow. I thought you might like to find something to do since you don't care to be around him."

"What gave you that idea?" It was true that she wasn't particularly fond of Ed, but she was sure she had never mentioned that fact to Vince.

He frowned as though trying to remember. "I'm not sure where I got that impression. Maybe he told me he didn't think you liked him."

"I don't dislike him."

"Ed occasionally brings along a friend."

A female friend, she gathered. Did Ed bring along a date for Vince, too? She was shocked by the surge of jealousy the thought aroused. "I'll be glad to disappear. Maybe May would like to go to the movies or something." She set the bowl down, and the dog quickly abandoned the food in favor of a drink, which he began slurping noisily.

Vince nodded, as his sightless gaze was drawn to the sounds the dog was making. "Have you given him a name yet?" he asked, stepping back but holding the screen door for her as she mounted the steps carrying the bag of dog food. His ability to pinpoint exactly where she was at any given moment was disconcerting.

"I haven't been able to come up with one. I thought I'd get to know him for a while before I decide." She glanced at him. "Any suggestions?"

"No," he answered too quickly.

"How do you like the name Bandit? I found him chewing on one of your deck shoes this morning. He had one of mine yesterday."

"Up to you."

She looked back out at the dog and shook her head. "No, not Bandit. It doesn't suit him."

"What color is he?"

"He's gold, of course. A golden retriever usually is." She looked outside again. "Actually, he's a very light gold. He's more the color of . . ." Frowning, she searched her mind for something the exact color. "Golden pound cake or sawdust or—"

He shrugged, drawing her attention to his broad shoulders. "Sawdust. That's a helluva name, but it's better than Dog."

"I like it," said A.J. But her thoughts were suddenly as far away from the dog as they could possibly be.

Vince was wearing a pair of jeans and a white polo shirt that had seen better days. The much-washed fabric defined the muscles in his arms and chest. She looked at him more closely. Was it her imagination or had he gained a couple of pounds since her arrival? She smiled to herself as she studied him. Her culinary efforts seemed to be reaping their reward. And she was sure she'd heard him using the exercise equipment in his bedroom.

She stopped in the mudroom to put the dog food away and wash her hands. He waited for her. Keeping her gaze on him, she tore off a piece of paper towel to dry her hands. "Vince, may I ask you something?"

she asked as she returned the jacket to the locker where she'd found it.

He stopped on his way to the hall. "Sure."

"Can you distinguish any light at all?"

He stiffened. "No," he said, his tone terse with anger. "I told you, Amanda, I have a convoy of doctors. I don't need another one." He turned on his heel and left her staring after him.

She pushed her hands into her hair, sighed deeply and went to call May. She explained about Ed's visit. "I thought I'd go shopping for apples tomorrow, have dinner out somewhere and take in a movie. Would you like to go with me?"

"I'd love to," said May with such delight that A.J. was glad she'd asked. "And I know the warehouses with the best prices and tastiest apples. Some of those places will charge you like a tourist if you aren't careful."

"I'll pick you up right after lunch."

A.J. had planned to be gone by the time Ed Wilson arrived. Unfortunately for her, he was early.

She heard his voice from downstairs. Odd, she hadn't noticed the sound of a car. "Drat," she said to herself as she pulled a red wool sweater that matched her slacks over her head. She smoothed her hair again.

This couldn't be a comfortable meeting. During that same summer years ago, she had witnessed a moment of weakness in Ed Wilson. She had found that people rarely forgave that.

She fiddled around in her room for a few minutes, hoping the two men would move out on the porch and she could get away without having to greet him.

But she could hear their voices in the main room, and at last she could postpone her departure no longer. She picked up her shoulder bag and left the room.

Ed spied her at the top of the steps and didn't take his eyes off her all the way down. She was edgy under his piercing stare but she forced herself to remain nonchalant. She decided to take the initiative. "How are you, Ed? I didn't hear your car."

"Yours was in the carport, so I parked behind the cabin."

When she reached the bottom, she approached the bar, where they both stood. "You're looking well," she said with an impersonal smile.

His movie-star handsomeness was far different from Vince's careless, more virile, good looks. But, as far as she was concerned, he was much less attractive.

"I'm fine, A.J." He took her hands and spread them wide as he looked at her. "It's been a long time since we were all together in Hawaii. And you! I don't even have to ask. You are spectacular. My, my." He shook his head as though he couldn't believe it. "Vince, it's a shame you can't see what a vision this woman has become."

What an unkind thing to say, she thought, looking quickly to Vince. But the remark didn't seem to have any effect on him.

"Thank you," she said coolly, then turned her back, ignoring him. "Vince, I forgot to get directions to May's house."

"She lives the next farm over, between here and town. I think it's about a mile down the road on the left. According to your dad, the house is yellow, with Victorian gingerbread."

"Thanks. I'm sure I can find it. See you later."

In the car, she thought back through the puzzling exchange. Ed was his usual charming self. He acted as though nothing had ever happened between them. She would have thought he'd treat her with reserve, at least, instead of strewing his elaborate compliments on her.

Maybe he really didn't remember the incident. Maybe he was one of those people who could put unpleasant events out of his mind until they were forgotten completely.

Now that she thought about it, she couldn't understand why Vince and Ed were such close friends, why Ed was the one who visited regularly. They hadn't been buddies when she'd known them. That was a long time ago, of course; but she couldn't imagine that the two of them had anything in common.

May was waiting on her front porch. "Hi," she said cheerfully. "What movie are we going to see?"

"I hadn't thought about it," A.J. said absently as she gazed at the house. It was meticulously maintained. "I like your house. It must be quite a job to keep up."

"It is, and it's far too much house for one person. But the place has been in my family so long, I'd feel guilty if I sold it. Your father helped me paint the trim one weekend this summer."

John? With a paintbrush in his hand? She had a hard time believing it of him. Once again, she thought of the influence this woman was having on her father.

May got in and snapped on her seat belt. "Do you like Mel Gibson?" she asked.

"He's okay," A.J. answered, her features in the same distracted expression.

When she didn't say anything further, May gave a disgusted shrug. "Honestly! Anyone who doesn't like Mel Gibson is un-American."

"What?" A.J. gave a rueful grin and apologized. "I'm sorry, May, I was thinking about something else. Besides, Mel Gibson is Australian. And I thought we'd get the apples first. Tell me which way to go."

May grinned. "Good to see you awake. Turn right at the second traffic light." She shifted in her seat. The older woman seemed to have something on her mind.

A.J. smiled encouragingly.

"I'm delighted to be asked, of course, but do you mind telling me what brought about this invitation?"

"Ed Wilson was coming. Vince suggested—in the nicest way—that I get lost."

May nodded. "I thought it might be something like that. Your father says you all knew each other years ago."

"Yes," A.J. replied cautiously. She didn't want to reveal her real feelings.

"Do you get along with Ed Wilson?"

A.J. shrugged.

"I suppose I should admire him for his loyalty to Vince," May said, a touch of acid in her voice. "For some reason, though, despite his impeccable manners, I dislike the man. John doesn't get it. It's probably some kind of male bonding thing that we're not supposed to understand."

A.J. laughed, but not for the reasons May would assume. This was a revealing conversation, and she'd like to keep it going. "I know what you mean." She hesitated. "You and my father know each other well, then?"

She was surprised to see May blush. And delighted when May answered, "Fairly well."

This woman was so different from her father's usual companions. "Maybe there's hope for him yet."

May blushed even redder. "Here's your turn," she said and put an end to the personal banter.

The Georgia apple season coincided with the changing of the leaves, so the traffic was unusually heavy. A.J. drove along the curving roads, through valleys, beside streams. May kept a lively conversation going, pointing out landmarks. They both were in awe of the spectacular fall color spectrum.

Traffic was heavy. Tourists flocked to the mountains each year in late October and continued to clog the highways until the first frost, usually around the third week in November. They came to the area to stock up on the tart crisp fruit in anticipation of traditional Thanksgiving and Christmas baking. The spin-off enterprises thrived, as well—homemade items such as apple jelly, apple syrup, apple butter, fried apple pies, apple bread, dried apples and apple relish disappeared off the warehouse shelves and wayside stands almost as fast as they were stocked.

The two women had to visit three places before May found the kind of apple bread she wanted. The smells were seductive, and A.J. bought samples of everything. When they'd finished, there was time for a quick dinner before the movie.

It was very late when A.J. dropped off May at the lovely old Victorian house.

"I had a wonderful time," said the older woman. "Thank you for asking me."

"Thank you for going," answered A.J. "Next time though, I want a tour of your house. How long has it been in your family?"

"Since 1867," May said, climbing out of the car. She leaned back in to say, "You're welcome to come in now."

"No, it's much too late tonight. Next time."

"Next time," May agreed. "You and Vince can come to dinner. What about next Wednesday night?"

"Has he ever been to your house?" A.J. asked. This might be the perfect solution to her dilemma. He might leave the house for May.

"Not once. I have asked repeatedly, but he always comes up with a convenient excuse."

"I had already made up my mind to push him about getting out of the cabin," A.J. mused. "If there's any way, we'll be there," she added, determined.

"You can talk him into it."

"Me?" She shook her head ruefully. "He pays no attention to me, May. I've tried to get him outside for exercise—"

May interrupted her. "Next time, don't think of yourself as a doctor when you try. Think of yourself as a woman. Make him want to be with you."

A.J.'s jaw went slack. Her face burned like someone with a temperature of a hundred and five. "He doesn't—we don't—"

May didn't change her expression. "Of course you don't. But you should. I've seen the way he follows your progress when you walk across a room." She chuckled. "I'd almost think he could see. He does need to get out, and you should use whatever weapons you have."

"I'll tell him you asked. Good night, May."

May had given her a mind full of things to think about as she drove back to the cabin. Unfortunately she reached the driveway too quickly to come to any conclusions.

The cabin was dark except for one light in the mudroom. The dog greeted her and kept her company as she put away her apple purchases and went upstairs, tiptoeing past Vince's door so she wouldn't wake him.

The dog left her there. He slept against the wall, out of Vince's path, but as close as he could get to the door.

When she had brushed her teeth and washed her face, she lay on her bed thinking about her day. And about May.

The trip had been quite revealing. Clearly May and John had been spending a lot of time together. A.J. was glad. May just might have the ability to humanize the man. She might be right for him.

But May was mistaken about Vince.

The next morning A.J. awoke to the sound of the furnace. She dressed in a bright pink warm-up suit and came downstairs early. As she passed Vince's door, the dog opened one eye to check that it was her, then closed it again.

The radio was playing softly in the background, and she was busy in the kitchen when she heard footsteps behind her. "I have to use some of these apples I

bought yesterday. How do apple pancakes sound to
you this morning?'' she asked.

"Sounds delicious," said a voice behind her.

Her hand went to her chest and she whirled to find
Ed Wilson in the doorway.

He smiled, displaying his very white, very large
teeth. "Sorry to startle you. I decided to spend the
night," he informed her unnecessarily.

"Of course. Fine." She looked past him. "Where's
Vince?"

"I heard the shower. He'll probably be down in a
minute." Ed settled himself comfortably at the pass-
through counter and gave her a thorough visual ex-
amination. Her warm-up was a size too big—she liked
them loose—but under his gaze her clothes felt tight.
He had ogled her last night, too, but then she hadn't
felt like things were crawling all over her. "It's been a
long time, A.J.," he said smoothly.

Not long enough. But she was determined that he
should not get a reaction out of her. "Yes, it has." She
turned up the volume on the radio, but it didn't deter
him.

"I remember that summer well. God, but you were
a pest." He grinned as though to take the sting out of
his words—but his eyes belied the effort. They were
cold, challenging her, daring her to comment. Well,
he'd answered her question. He hadn't forgotten a
thing about that last night.

"I'm sure I was," she answered, gritting her teeth
until her jaw ached.

"You thought you were in love with Vince that
summer, didn't you?" he asked, waving a hand toward the ceiling to indicate that he was referring to the

man upstairs. "You almost drove the poor man crazy. He used to say you were sixteen years old going on twenty-five. We were laughing about that just last night."

Why did that hurt? She had been a child; she shouldn't still care.

He smiled at her expression. "And when you couldn't get Vince to pay attention to you, you turned to me."

Ed behaved as though he was deliberately baiting her. As though he wanted her to get angry. Why? Shaking her head in disbelief, she crossed her arms and leaned one hip against the counter. The blatant lie was the proverbial straw. She couldn't let him get away with such an allegation. "Ed, one of us has a badly defective memory. Except for a few dances one disastrous night, I never spent more than five minutes in your company." Thoughts of that night sent a shiver across her shoulders.

He persisted pleasantly. "That's not the way I remember it."

Then she shrugged. "Think what you want," she told him dismissively. She'd vowed to put away all regrets from fourteen years ago, and she was going to stick to the vow. "I understand from my father that you've been very loyal to Vince since the crash, that you've visited him regularly and driven him when he needed to go in for tests. I'm sure he's grateful for your support. Were you in Saudi Arabia with him?"

He nodded and for a brief moment looked uncomfortable. Then he gave her his broad smile again. The opening of the pass-through framed his handsome face and broad shoulders. She wondered if he realized the effect. Probably.

"Tell me about yourself. Vince says you're a doctor."

A.J. returned to beating the pancake batter. "That's right. But I wouldn't be any help to you, Ed. I'm not a psychiatrist." Drat. She shouldn't have said that.

His eyes narrowed dangerously. She felt a tremor of apprehension pass across her shoulders. Crazy. Why should she be afraid? She turned away to check that the griddle was hot.

When she heard Vince on the stairs, she poured out the pancake batter, enough for the two of them. She certainly wasn't going to sit down with this man.

"'Morning, Amanda," Vince said. He slid onto the other stool.

"Good morning," A.J. answered curtly. The cakes bubbled, she flipped them and in only minutes served the two plates she had warming in the oven.

"I've taken your portion, haven't I?" Ed's tone was unctuous with regret, but that unpleasant smile remained on his face. "Please, come and sit down, A.J. I can get something on my way out of town."

God, the man sounded so sincere. She'd love to wipe that oily smile off his face with the palm of her hand, preferably doubled into a fist. "Don't be silly, Ed. There's plenty of food here," she told him. "You may as well eat."

Vince's head swiveled between the two of them. His frown, however, was directed at A.J. "Is there a problem?" he asked.

"No problem at all," she said. Sawdust had followed Vince downstairs, giving her a good excuse to get out of there before she said something dreadful. She flicked the switch on the radio, plunging the room into silence. "I'm going to take the dog for a walk," she said and left.

She had covered only a short distance when a thought suddenly occurred to her. Did Ed want to drum up antagonism between them? Her footsteps faltered at the thought. She couldn't imagine why. But she knew what would happen to the fragile progress she'd made if she were to complain to Vince.

She had no intention of doing so. A complaint would serve no purpose except to drive a wedge between them. Vince would naturally stick up for his buddy. She couldn't blame him for that; from all she'd heard Ed had been a good friend since the crash.

Besides, she was perfectly able to hold her own in any altercation with the man...*if* she ever saw him again.

Vince had been aware of the strain in the atmosphere between them this morning. He would make sure she was warned when Ed was coming.

Sawdust jerked on the leash to remind her of their purpose.

Ed had little to say on the subject of Amanda Upton.

Vince tried to pry, in a tactful way, into what had happened this morning. What had been going on between the two of them? When he came downstairs he could feel Amanda's antagonism like heat simmering inside her. Ed had caused it, he was sure.

He had been Ed's squadron leader for two years before the crash. In that capacity he'd learned that, in order to get the most from the man, he needed to handle him correctly. Ed was a good leader, a great pilot—but if he was in a disagreeable mood, it was better to walk away. His moods never lasted long, he always seemed to recover quickly and he never sulked, thank God.

Today there was a hostile undertone in Ed's voice, one he probably wasn't aware of, when he had denied that he'd argued with Amanda. "I barely know the woman," he had grumbled. "What would we have argued about?"

Vince supposed he'd have to take his friend's word for it. But *something* had been going on. There had been enough friction in the atmosphere between them to kindle a fire with wet wood. He wanted answers.

Ed left a few minutes later to return to the base north of Atlanta.

Over the noise of Ed's car engine, Vince heard his own sigh. The sound was crowded with relief. In addition to the remarkable mood Ed was in, his friend had spent the afternoon yesterday talking about his latest blond conquest, the shows they'd seen together in Atlanta, the new restaurants where they'd dined and the hot "in" clubs where they'd danced. He knew Ed tried hard to be a good friend, helping where he could during this hellacious time, but his visits always left Vince feeling depressed as hell.

Vince didn't want his friend and this woman who'd been foisted on him by her well-meaning father at each other's throats. The doctors had listed the things he needed for recovery: plenty of rest—he'd certainly had that; exercise—admittedly he could use more of that;

and a stress-free environment—which he'd had until Amanda's arrival.

Aw, hell. He raked his hair with restless fingers. Amanda was okay. He wouldn't have complained too loudly before this morning. She'd been here a week today. As requested, she had left him alone, more or less. And she was a great cook.

She hadn't returned from her walk. Vince washed the few breakfast dishes and wandered through the downstairs. The cabin seemed so empty, so quiet, without her. He turned the radio on. When she was around, she usually kept it playing in the background. Her favorite music seemed to be rhythm and blues or jazz, sweet and hot. Odd that their tastes in music were similar.

He moved around the room, fidgety, edgy. He couldn't seem to settle down this morning.

Amanda and Ed. Had his friend made a pass at her?

Vince stopped beside the back of a chair and wrapped his fingers tightly around the top rung. He was surprised at how much he disliked that idea.

He was waiting by the door when Amanda entered the house moments later. "Did Ed Wilson come on to you?" he demanded.

"Heavens, no," she answered instantly.

The dog moved between them; he felt the brush against his leg. Impatient, he bent to remove the leash from the dog's collar, releasing him. When he straightened again he continued. "There was something going on. Something that made him uncomfortable ... or guilty. And you dashed out of here so fast, you were almost rude."

She hesitated. "Let me ask you something. Did you and Ed discuss me after I left yesterday?"

"No."

"Then I must have misunderstood something he said. It's nothing."

Vince felt his anger build—anger born of frustration and directed at himself more than Ed or her. At one time he could decipher people's feelings from their expressions, and he was usually correct. He still could if he could just *see* her. "Tell me," he grated.

"Ed was talking to me about that last night in Hawaii. As you know, it's an uncomfortable subject for me," she said finally, after a long pause.

Vince froze. Her answer was the last thing he'd expected. Until Ed had mentioned Hawaii this morning, Vince had forgotten he was also stationed there that summer. "What does Ed know about that night?"

She hesitated again. When she spoke he realized she'd moved away from him. "Not much. If you want details, you'll have to ask him."

He heard her feet on the steps and strode quickly to the newel post, lifting his head toward her. "I'm asking you, damn it."

"Well, I'm not answering." She spoke from the top of the stairs.

He slapped the banister with his open hand, the sound like a shot, the action stinging his palm.

At the end of the upstairs hall, a door slammed.

From beside him, Vince heard the dog whine.

A.J. knew Vince was still irritated with her. Well, that made them even. She was irritated, too. He needn't think she was going to be drawn into an argument over Ed Wilson. She was preparing dinner, and as usual the radio was playing soft music from a local station. Suddenly an announcer broke in with the news of another fire. She increased the volume and listened to the details. But there was nothing new in the story. The police were still stymied, said the announcer.

Something bothered her—some niggling impression played around in the back of her mind. But she couldn't put her finger on what it was. Vince came downstairs for dinner, and she set the worry aside to be examined later. They were both silent during most of the meal.

When Vince did finally speak, his words—and his tone—shocked her. He put down his fork, wiped his mouth with his napkin and pushed his plate back. Then he crossed his arms on the surface in front of him. "Ed has been a good friend to me, especially since the crash, but I recognize that he has some faults. He's often impatient and too outspoken."

The very mildness of his statement took her by surprise. There was something else in his voice, a hint of huskiness, that made her heart beat faster. "I told you, it's nothing I can't handle, Vince."

He turned toward her, swiveling his stool. His heels were hooked over the footrest and he rested his hands on his jeans-clad thighs. "If he made you uncomfortable, whether it was this morning or years ago, I want to know about it. Will you tell me?"

A.J. put down her fork. She twisted her stool, facing him as though pulled in his direction by a magnet. "Probably not," she admitted.

When he would have objected, she laid her hand on his. "Vince, if Ed told you that I didn't like him, he was only partially right. He irritates me at times but I can certainly get along with him. And I don't intend to be the cause of conflict between the two of you. Please don't ask me to do that."

He turned his hand and grasped her fingers. His hand was warm and strong. She felt the electricity all the way to her toes.

"I want to take your hair down."

Before she could answer he was standing over her. "Your hair was beautiful, the color of strong black coffee. And thick and wild."

"It's still wild. Vince, stop!"

He pulled at the confining pins. Before she could react, the mass tumbled down her back. He gathered handfuls of hair, lifting it off her neck, combing gently through the tangles with his fingers. At last, he spread it across her shoulders. "There," he said. "You said you needed time off. This will help you think of yourself as a woman rather than a doctor for a while."

She recalled May saying the same thing to her. What was this, a conspiracy? "That's insulting. I do think of myself as a woman." She started to lift her arms, to twist the hair back again.

"Leave it." Vince halted her movement by cupping her face in his big hands. "You still use the same shampoo," he muttered.

Her brows shot up. Good grief, had he said what she thought he said?

He was on his feet and she remained perched on the stool, so he had to lean down to catch her mouth beneath his. There was a desperation in the move, as though he had fought against, but lost out to, a need for human contact.

A.J. was too stunned to react for a moment. The kiss was unexpected. His lips were firm, mobile and very knowing. His tongue demanded entrance. She made a sound—was it a moan? Suddenly the kiss exploded into hungry passion like none she'd ever known.

She was lifted off the stool and into his arms, her toes barely skimming the floor, her body molded from breast to knees against his. His open hands spread across her back, exerting pressure to hold her against him. His tongue, having gained its objective, swept into her mouth, exploring hungrily and unhesitatingly.

Her arms had circled his waist—for balance, she told herself. Her fingers gripped his shirt, as her body strained toward his glorious heat.

Then he was gone. Her feet were flat on the floor. Her arms were empty.

"I'm sorry, Amanda," he muttered, wiping his mouth with the back of his hand.

"Yes," she said softly, hearing the break in her voice. His kiss had left her reeling. She cleared her throat and caught sight of herself reflected in his glasses. Was that her, that sappy-looking female with the dreamy eyes and silly smile? "Well," she said, more strongly. She squared her shoulders. "Yes."

"I've apologized, damn it." He spun on his heel, hesitated briefly to get his bearings and then left the room.

A.J. sat back on the stool. Her legs felt like limp noodles. One thing about Vince Thornborough hadn't changed at all. He was still the sexiest, most exciting man she'd ever encountered.

Upstairs, Vince straddled the bench of the weight machine. He gripped the cold metal bars and lifted. Again and again he shoved the bar over his head. He began to breathe hard. Sweat broke out over his face and body, and he even groaned a bit. A muscle in his shoulder protested with a biting pain.

The taste of Amanda, the miracle of her soft skin, the sensation of her loose hair tangled around his fingers had shaken Vince to his foundation.

The kiss was a stupid, impulsive move, he told himself firmly, which wouldn't be repeated.

He thought he'd been handling his life fairly well—he'd learned to get by alone in these familiar surroundings. He didn't need more than a minimum of help.

Now he had to admit to a host of shadowy thoughts and fears. He had discovered, unexpectedly, that he wasn't the strong, self-controlled, cocky son of a bitch he'd thought he was.

Chapter 5

May brought the mail in on Monday morning. "Six letters for Dr. Upton. Two bills for Major Thornborough."

"Story of my life," Vince said wryly from the overstuffed chair where he sat. The weather was too cold for the porch this morning. Except for a rare day, it would probably be too cold until spring.

Amanda entered from the kitchen where she'd been doing laundry. "Thanks, May. Help yourself to coffee."

"I will, thanks."

"Are those the answers you've been waiting for?" Vince asked Amanda, his tone detached. He'd tried to put the memory of last night's kiss out of his mind, but he hadn't been successful. The sooner she found a job and left here, the better off he would be.

"Five of them are," she said, shuffling through the pile. "The sixth is a letter from my mother."

"To urge you again to move to Florida?"

"More than likely." She dropped the other letters on a table and tore into that envelope. She scanned the letter. "Well, no," she said after a moment, delight in her voice. "Just the opposite. My brothers are being considered for tennis scholarships at the University of Georgia. Now Mother has decided it will be nice that I live close and can keep an eye on them."

"I didn't know you had brothers," said May as she entered, carrying a cup of steaming coffee.

A.J. grinned at her. "They're my half brothers. Carlton and David are terrific kids, though I didn't always think so, did I, Vince?" she added, throwing him a quick glance. "They're eleven years younger than I am, identical twins. And they *are* bang-up tennis players, thus the scholarships."

Vince couldn't resist asking, "Better than you?"

"Much better," she pronounced.

He rested his head against the back of his chair. "Then I sure as hell don't ever want to play them."

"Mother sent pictures, too." A.J. acted before she thought, extending the pictures toward Vince.

Realizing the futility of the gesture, A.J. bit her lip and exchanged a poignant glance with May. Then May took the pictures. "Nice-looking boys," she said.

Vince was struck by the emotion in Amanda's voice when she talked about her brothers. There was much he didn't know about this woman, he reminded himself. She had grown up with the same people, lived in the same town, for years. She had gone to high school, had best friends that she giggled with, boyfriends she dated. "Describe your brothers to me," he requested quietly.

"Well, let me see—they are tall, over six feet. They get that from their father. They have the most gorgeous blond hair and their eyes are dark. The only difference between them is that they're mirror images, Carlton is left- and David is right-handed."

"Good Lord, they must play terrific doubles."

A.J. laughed, that wonderful musical sound that made him smile. Suddenly he would have given ten years of his life to be able to see her, to watch her eyes sparkle, to look for the dimple that played in her cheek when she was happy.

The darkness had never seemed so black. He closed his hand into a fist and cleared his throat of the emotion there. When he spoke, his tone was casual. "May, you wouldn't believe this pint-size woman when she gets on a tennis court. I swear she grows six inches and takes on the personality of a very aggressive tiger."

"I come by the aggression naturally," A.J. explained to May. "Maybe John told you—my mother began playing professional tennis when she was fifteen." May shook her head and she continued. "Jane never made it to the big-time tournaments, but tennis is still her greatest passion.

"I'm afraid I was a major disappointment to her— I wasn't interested in playing tennis for a living. But now she coaches the boys. Maybe they'll help her fulfill her dream."

The three of them were lost in their own thoughts for a moment. The room was quiet.

Finally May broke the silence. "Well, Vince, have we put off paying the bills long enough?" she said finally.

Vince placed his hands on the arms of his chair. "Yes, let's get started on them."

"I need to call some of these places to confirm appointments," said A.J. "I'll use the phone in the kitchen."

Vince picked up the cordless telephone from the table next to him. "Why don't you take this?"

It would be quieter and more comfortable upstairs, she thought. "Okay, thanks. I'll be in my room."

"A.J., have you thought about talking to the hospitals here in town?" May asked. "We have two."

A.J. was taken aback by the question. Here? Living in the same town with her father? "Well, no, I hadn't," she admitted. "I'm not sure the community could handle two Uptons, are you, Vince?" she asked, trying to make it into an amusing statement.

"I don't think you ought to exclude this town just because John will be living here."

A.J. stared at him, then shrugged. "I'll give them a call." It couldn't hurt. She didn't actually have to make an appointment.

She rose to leave, but May stopped her with another question. "Did you ask Vince about coming to dinner Wednesday night?"

A.J. had forgotten. This was ridiculous—she never forgot things.

She tried to forgive her lapse, blaming it on the surprise of finding Ed still here Sunday morning, the argument with Vince and the breath-stealing memory of his kiss. She'd not fallen asleep until the wee hours of this morning.

She realized that, rather than finding a comfortable place to lay the blame, she was merely stirring the unsettling memory into fiery life once again. "I'm sorry, May."

"Well, I'm asking now. Vince, will you come to my house for dinner on Wednesday?"

Vince was surprised by the invitation. May knew that he only left the cabin when it was a necessity.

He was also surprised by Amanda's reaction. Curiously, she'd waited a long time to answer. And when the answer came, her voice was thick with some rich emotion that he couldn't place.

His first inclination was to refuse the invitation outright. He confused himself by hedging. "I don't know..."

"You can have some time to think about it," May announced. "Let's get busy."

A.J. left, taking the cordless receiver with her, and the room was silent except for the sounds of shuffling papers as May finished writing the checks and addressing envelopes. "There. All done for another month," she said finally. She got to her feet. "Do you need anything from town?"

"Yes, we do. I'll give you a list." He stopped. "Let me ask you something first."

"Certainly." She sat down again.

"How does Amanda...?" He wasn't sure how to put this. "What do you...? Aw, hell—it's damn hard to talk when you can't see the person you're talking to." He raked impatient fingers through his hair. "I guess what I mean is, do you *like* her?"

"I like her very much," she answered, sounding surprised. "I really enjoyed spending the day with her on Saturday. She treated me as a contemporary, rather than the old woman I am." She broke off, chuckling. "That's a stellar example of her compassion. She's good company, too. Like a friend." She paused again and the silence stretched out. "Kind is a good, old-fashioned word. A.J. is kind."

"She wasn't always kind." The bitterness seeped in.

"Yes, I've heard of the infamous summer in Hawaii."

"From her?" he demanded.

"Of course not," she said with some asperity. "You need to learn to trust her, Vince. No, I heard the story from John." Her voice took on a musing tone. "He says he was at a loss as to how to handle her, which doesn't surprise me. From what I gather, he was a good commander, but he didn't have a suitable expertise with teenage girls. One doesn't manage them. They have to be nudged and guided carefully along the right path."

Vince hadn't thought of it before, but now he remembered that May taught in high school. She would know a lot about teens. "John tried," he said, defending his friend.

"Oh, yes, I'm quite sure he did. But now that I know about her rejection of her mother's ambition for her, I think she must have been an extremely lonely child. How old was she?"

"Sixteen, but she was no child, believe me." He hesitated, remembering the lush curves, the flirtatious routine. Then, superimposed over that memory was one of himself, called on the carpet by John, his commanding officer and his friend. Accused of contributing to the delinquency of a minor. Even after he'd been cleared, there were those who kept their distance for quite a while, including John. "It would be hard for me to ever trust Amanda."

"Let me ask you something," May said sharply.

"Shoot."

"Don't tempt me," she muttered as an aside. "You seem to like A.J. well enough most of the time. In fact, you're more than interested, you're attracted to her. Obviously you can't see her, Vince, but your head turns in her direction, your attention follows her wherever she goes."

"That's bull—"

She cut him off quickly. "There's nothing wrong with those feelings. Why shouldn't you be attracted to her? She's a lovely young woman. Intelligent, educated, entertaining."

Abruptly Vince's heart ballooned in his chest. He couldn't sit still any longer. He got to his feet and, shoving one hand in the pocket of his jeans, began to pace the empty trail he'd arranged behind the sofa.

"Let's say you were right, May. Say I *was* interested—in any woman." He stopped, gestured with his free hand, palm up. "What would I have to offer someone who is educated and entertaining? Say I asked her for a date. I suppose she could lead me into a fine restaurant, read the menu out loud, cut up my meat for me. And afterward, she could lead me by the hand into the theater and explain what was happening onstage. She would even have to lead on a dance floor. Do you think that would be pleasant for any woman? Hell, no."

He resumed his pacing. "I know that hundreds of thousands of people learn to live full lives with my problem. But they're not me. I'm not fooling myself any longer. The doctors expected some improvement before now. They thought I would have been able to discern light or movement. I can't see a damn thing but *black*. I don't even know where I go from here. All I've ever done, all I've ever known, was flying and the military."

His steps slowed; his voice dropped to a muffled undertone as he relived yesterday's kiss, Amanda's soft lips, her sweet taste. "What the *hell* do I have to offer her?"

"Maybe more than you think."

The pain in his chest increased, threatened to suffocate him. He took off his glasses for a minute, turning away so she couldn't read the emotion on his face. He tilted his head back and blinked hard to keep the moisture in his eyes from falling, from becoming tears. Hell, he was a grown man. Men didn't cry. "You're wrong," he said finally, replacing the glasses.

"That is the most insulting soliloquy I've ever heard in my life," said May.

He whipped his head around. "Insulting?"

"To any woman," she explained. "Particularly A.J. Since she isn't here to take offense, I shall take offense for her. Do you really consider her so shallow?"

"I don't know her that well," he said stiffly, realizing that it was a weak argument but taken aback by May's attack.

May had risen—he heard her approach until she stood directly in front of him. "She made mistakes when she was young. Give her some leeway. Teenagers have a rough time of it, you know, under the best of conditions and in every generation. At sixteen my own mother wanted to drown me in the creek behind our house. She told me so. I'd be willing to gamble that at sixteen, you were no great shakes, either."

The silence was heavy and thick with her indignation. Vince fought a smile as he felt the frustration and regret drain out of him, felt the suffocating pain around his heart ease.

He'd never seen May, but he could picture her now, a bantam hen fighting for her chick. "You'd be right. Thanks, May," he ended quietly.

"For what?"

"I was feeling sorry for myself, getting pretty morose, wasn't I?"

Silence greeted his words. "You're allowed," she said finally, softly. He heard the huskiness in her voice and opened his mouth to deny her sympathy.

But suddenly he felt her arms around him, hugging him tightly. He caught his breath in astonishment. Such a physical gesture of affection was an unfamiliar sensation. Oh, he'd taken the masculine back-slapping, the enthusiastic hand-pumpings, even a quick hard clasp from a pal. But a purely affectionate gesture, nothing sexual attached—he didn't remember the last time he'd experienced such an event. His mother had died when he was a small child. His father had certainly never hugged him.

For a moment Vince stiffened at the strange warmth, feeling restricted and apprehensive. Then he let out a long sigh and returned the hug, laying his forehead against May's. Her generous but undemanding attention felt good, so good. He relaxed. A moment passed. Another.

At last, in an attempt to lighten the atmosphere, he said, "You're taller than I thought you were."

She gave a choked laugh. "Tall enough to handle you, bub," she joked unsteadily.

He gave her another squeeze and released her. They didn't speak again of A.J. or of his handicap.

Vince dictated a shopping list, and they discussed some work she thought needed to be done outside, to get the place ready for winter.

"The storm last week knocked some tree branches down," she told him. "They need to be hauled away."

"John said to do whatever work needed to be done. And Amanda mentioned that the drive needed to be spread with a load of gravel."

She laughed. "It certainly does. I'll find someone to take care of all this. And I'll expect the two of you at my house Wednesday night at seven?"

He thought for a minute. "All right."

Amanda was still on the telephone when May left with his list in her hand. "I have a meeting of the historical society. If you don't need any of these things before then, I'll be by around six."

"That's fine," he told her.

He could hear Amanda's voice from upstairs but not the words. He was tempted to listen in—he hadn't been convinced when she first arrived that she really was job hunting.

He was relaxed, almost dozing, when he felt a wet nose on his hand. "Hi, Sawdust," he said, scratching behind the dog's ear. But that wasn't what the creature wanted. It took him a minute to get the message. "You want to go out."

The quick click of nails as the dog danced on the floor told him he'd been correct.

"I can't take you. I don't even know where the leash is."

A soft whine was the only response he got.

Vince heaved a sigh. "You're a lot of trouble, you know it?" He went into the kitchen and felt around in all the places where she might keep the leash. At last he found it hanging from the handle of a drawer. He snapped it to the dog's collar. "Your name ought to be Trouble. Okay, let's go."

They went through the porch. Vince hesitated at the door leading outside. He rarely ventured beyond this point; he felt the most vulnerable when he was out of doors.

From the time he was old enough to think and reason, Vince had resolved to always be in command of himself. That was why he didn't drink anything stronger than an occasional beer and had never been tempted to experiment with drugs as many of his contemporaries did. This situation was doubly difficult to tolerate for the kind of man he was.

The fears were there. They dwelt within him, no matter how much he might try to deny them or rationalize their insignificance. Those fears were why he didn't go farther than the porch. The fear that he would get lost, that he would become disoriented and not be able to find the cabin again. The fear that something or someone would come out of the forest and catch him unaware and unprepared. He would never admit it to a soul—he hadn't even told Ed—but he was scared spitless without a roof over his head.

"If you drag me into the lake, you're dead meat," he said to Sawdust.

But the dog led him through the grass and fallen pine needles directly onto the path which had been cut around the lake. "Good boy," he said when he felt the smooth path beneath his feet. "I believe I can handle this, as long as we don't go too far." He heard the animation in his own voice, the energy and vigor that had been missing for far too long. He felt good. But he kept a firm hand on the leash.

They walked slowly, pausing occasionally. The sunlight was warm on his head. He liked the sound of leaves and pine needles under his feet. The air was crisp and clean, a refreshing change. He smelled pine and cedar and began to relax.

Finally the dog reversed their course and headed back in the direction of the cabin. They had just stepped back inside—Vince leaned down to unsnap the leash—when A.J. came down the steps.

"You took Sawdust out?" she asked, the disbelief patent in her voice. He straightened, and she took the last few steps on the run. "Oh, Vince," she enthused as she hugged him. "That's great! That's wonderful! Thank you."

When she would have pulled back, he looped his hands together behind her back and grinned. "Great and wonderful, huh? So Sawdust is your dog, and you're going to do everything for him? He won't pester me or get in my way. I wouldn't be surprised if you had been hiding up there, waiting and watching."

Her hands rested on his shoulders, and she used one to give him a mock punch. "Hush. He *is* my dog. But I'm glad he got you to go outside. Didn't it feel good to walk on pine needles and have a lake breeze on your face?"

"Yeah, it felt good." He laughed huskily. "Not half as good as what you're doing right now, though."

A.J. became very still as she felt his arousal against her belly. Heated blood thickened and began to pump heavily through her veins, slowing motion and perception. What started as an affectionate cuddle had suddenly changed into an erotic embrace. She couldn't say that it was completely unexpected. After the kiss they'd shared yesterday, she should have been more cautious about touching him.

His reaction to yesterday's interlude was still a mystery to her. He had clearly been as shaken as she, but his desire had quickly turned to regret. "Do you want to let go of me?" she asked.

"Not a chance," he muttered as his mouth came down to cover hers.

She parted her lips in welcome. Rising on tiptoe, she slid her hands up around his neck, and buried her fingers in his thick hair.

Vince's hands moved restlessly up and down her back, molding the soft pliable curves of her body against the planes of his. He cradled her breast in his hand, provoking an enticing moan from deep within her throat. Where their bodies touched, the heat was intense, but when he heard the soft sound, heat wasn't enough for Vince. He circled her body with his arms to lift her off her feet. He angled his face to get a closer seal on their lips. He had no idea how long they kissed.

Finally, when they both had to have air, he wrenched his mouth away and buried his face in her neck, taking long deep breaths to replenish his starving lungs. "Oh, Lord, Amanda."

The episode had happened so quickly, been so fiery, and taken him by such surprise that he couldn't think clearly. He could only feel, and against her flat belly he felt hard and hungry and alive. And jubilant.

It took a moment, too, for it to dawn on him that she was trying to loosen his grip. She was so tiny, and his hold on her had been tight. He responded instantly. "Dear God, did I hurt you?"

"No, no. You didn't hurt me, Vince. Don't you hear—"

He didn't let her finish. He covered her lips once more in a brief kiss. Then, reluctantly, he let her feet touch the floor, her body separate from his. His fingers lingered at her waist, unwilling to let go.

"The dog," she said breathlessly.

Was it his imagination, or was she clinging to him, as well? At last he heard it—the dog barking from the back of the house, over the noise of an engine, which was immediately killed. Then a car door. Damn. He rested his forehead against hers and laughed unsteadily under his breath as he fought off his massive regret. "I didn't hear a thing," he admitted.

Her own laugh was equally shaky. "What? The man with ears like a bat?" she teased.

"I was diverted."

The sound of the bell separated them completely. The dog started barking. "Shall I get it?" she asked.

"Yeah, thanks," he said, grateful for the interval she was giving him to rein in his desire. She left the room with Sawdust on her heels.

By the time she returned with the sheriff, Vince was under control.

"Vince, it's the sheriff."

He got to his feet, extended his hand. "Sheriff White, how are you?" he said.

"Fine, Major," the sheriff answered in his slow, mountain drawl. He gripped Vince's hand firmly but briefly. "I'm sorry to have to barge in on you like this. I hope I'm not interrupting anything."

"Not a thing." Vince imagined Amanda biting back a smile. Or a frown.

"We had us another one of those fires yesterday, Major. Bigger than the others," he explained.

"I'm sorry, Sheriff," answered Vince. "Do you still think it's the kids?"

"Could be, could be a stranger bent on mischief. We get a lot of tourists this time of year, what with the apples comin' in and the leaves turnin'. Well, whoever's settin' them, our local fire department can't deal with it. This last fire worked its way onto U.S. Forest Service land. That brought them into the investigation right fast. Arson on that land is a federal offense, so now I really hope it ain't the kids."

Vince nodded, concerned in earnest now that the sheriff had actually proclaimed it arson. If the fires were spreading, if the kids didn't set them, the Forest Service would have better resources to deal with the problem.

The sheriff went on. "I'm trying to get around to all the folks that live on the outskirts of town, to put you on guard. So far they've been in uninhabited areas but that could change, or the fire could spread too quick for us.'' The sheriff scratched his head, dislodging his hat. He settled it firmly on his head again. ''The undergrowth is still pretty dry around here. That one storm we had a week or so ago wasn't enough to wet it down good. There's a lot of dead wood around, too.''

Vince nodded. ''May mentioned that today. She's looking for someone to clean up the broken limbs around the lake.''

''Good. I wanted to remind y'all of the danger of a forest fire—there just ain't no rhyme or reason to the way they burn. And I wanted to ask you if you'd be on the lookout for any strangers in the neighborhood.'' Suddenly he realized what he'd said. ''I mean... uh—''

Vince shook his head and gave the man a reassuring half smile. ''No offense taken, Sheriff. Dr. Upton has excellent vision. And the dog would probably warn us.''

''Yeah, a dog's a good idea. I'll leave you, then. You prob'ly oughtta keep your radio tuned to the local station, and remember to call if you see any strangers. I'll check them out.''

''We'll do that, Sheriff,'' said Amanda. ''Thank you for coming by.'' She walked out with him, caught up again with the niggling hunch in the back of her mind, the one she couldn't put her finger on. She should be able to figure it out by now.

At the back door the sheriff hesitated, glancing back to the hallway through which they'd come. ''Is there something else we need to know, Sheriff?'' she asked.

He spoke in an undertone, almost a whisper, that she had to lean close to hear. "May and my wife are good friends. I hope you won't take this as gossip, but she told us that you were lookin' for a job in the area and might be takin' some short trips."

"That's right."

"If you're gonna be gone overnight, Dr. Upton, you might wanna tell May so she can keep an especial eye out for the major."

"I'll do that, Sheriff," she promised. She stood at the door and waved as he left.

She came back to the main room to find Vince pacing, the hard look back on his face. She could clearly see that he'd worked himself into a rare temper. She paused on the threshold, wondering what on earth had happened in such a short time.

"The sheriff had something else to say, didn't he?" he demanded, jerking his head toward the back door. "Was he warning you not to leave me here alone?"

"Vince—"

"Was he?" he persisted.

"No," she said slowly. "But he did suggest that as a precautionary measure I let May know when I'm going to be out of town overnight. That seems like a practical idea to me."

"Yeah." Vince relented. He raked his fingers through his hair impatiently. "I'm sorry, Amanda. I could hear the two of you whispering at the door." He flung out an arm and resumed his pacing.

"I will *never* get used to people whispering. Never. I don't care what they say about me. I can handle remarks about blindness, I can even handle crude jokes about it, but I can't stand secrecy or subterfuge. I can't stand people who think they know what's best for me whispering and plotting behind my back. I'm going to be in on any decision. And I'm going to have my say."

A.J. stared at him for a long minute as her empathy reached out to him. And she understood. She was suddenly dismayed.

Of *course* he would hate for people to whisper about him. His ears were also his eyes.

How could she have been so thoughtless? She should have known. She should have had the insight to see . . . her head came up. She spoke in a clear, firm voice. "I don't blame you a bit for being angry, Vince. Whispering behind my back would make me very angry, too. I'm so sorry, I wasn't thinking. . . ."

Suddenly, unexpectedly, her eyes filled. What was the matter with her? She couldn't, she wouldn't cry, not today. "I promise never again to talk about you when you can't hear." The last few words began to break up, and she hoped he didn't notice. "I *promise,*" she whispered fiercely. Adamantly, she pressed her lips together, shook her head. He must not hear her cry; he would think her distress was born of pity.

But despite her will, despite her determination, tears escaped to splash down her cheeks. She wiped them away with a quick, rough swipe.

At her words, Vince came to a halt in front of her. He stood completely still, only inches away, focused with a fixed intensity, as though with only the strength of his need he could compel his blind eyes to see her.

He reached up and wrenched off the glasses. His face tightened into a concerned expression. "Amanda . . ."

A.J. looked into those beautiful brown eyes and felt his emotions added to hers—all the anguish, all the doubt and agony, all the fears, all the suffering he'd known since the crash. It hurt her. Dear God, did she still care for him?

She didn't think she could bear this. She took a deep breath and touched a shaking hand to her forehead. She wanted to help Vince, but, added to her own grim memories, the responsibility just might be too heavy right now. Furthermore, she'd promised herself some time before she faced and dealt with her own burnout. Her entire body began to tremble. It seemed her time had run out.

Vince touched her cheek, felt the wetness there and moaned. "Ah, damn, I made you cry." Abruptly he pulled her into his arms, enfolding her trembling body with his long arms. "Don't," he said hoarsely against her face. "Please, Amanda, I can't stand it if you cry."

"It wasn't you. These aren't tears of pity. I wouldn't have hurt you for the world, but I don't pity you, not one iota. You are the strongest man I know. You can, by God, take *care* of yourself. It's me."

She moved her head against his arm and the heavy coil of her hair came tumbling down over his hands, his arms. He caught his breath as the scent of shampoo reached his nostrils.

"I shouldn't ask, but you were my good friend once. I need someone to lean on just for a little while. Please." She wrapped her arms around his neck. Her body sagged against his as she sobbed.

Instantly he gave her the support she'd requested. Her whiskey voice sounded rusty as it dropped to a soft murmur. "Thank you. I'm tired, Vince. I need some of your strength. I know this is simply a classic case of burnout, but I can't shake the images of the hospital. I've lived with them for three years—the knifings, the fatal diseases, the addicts and alcoholics, the children—oh, Vince, the children. The past few years have been like living in hell."

His arms tightened. "God, Amanda, I never thought. I'm a selfish bastard. I've been so wound up in my own trouble... Hell!" He swung her up into his arms and crossed unerringly to the sofa. He sat, holding her across his lap, his arms warm and strong. He crooned soothing words, frivolous words. He ran his hand down the long, smooth mass of her hair. If she thought he was powerful enough to help her, to support her, then she could take whatever she needed from him.

For this woman he would give freely. His hand stilled on her back. He wasn't sure where that last thought had come from, but he would examine his motives later.

At last, A.J.'s sobbing ceased and her breathing leveled out. She started to apologize, and he hushed her. "Don't say you're sorry. Do you realize you're the first person who's asked anything of me in a long time, Amanda? I wish I could tell you how good it feels. We'll hash out all the explanations later."

"Okay." She relaxed, like a boneless, shapeless mass with no nerves, no muscles, in his arms. She felt secure for the first time in so long... maybe forever.

"You know," she murmured softly against his broad chest, "I used to wish I could turn off being a doctor. You and May said the same thing to me—be a woman, not a doctor. Like a switch or a faucet, I wanted to simply turn it off and rest for a while. But I can't.''

He had to lean close to hear her. He laid his lips against her temple. His breath was warm. "I was wrong. And if May said that, she was wrong, too. You could no more turn off being a doctor than you could turn off being a beautiful woman."

She tilted her head back and looked up at him. He hadn't replaced the glasses and though he couldn't see her, she had the feeling that he was looking with his other senses, or perhaps his soul could see what his eyes couldn't. "You *do* understand, don't you?"

At her question a ghost of a smile crossed his face. "I hope I do. If I'd noticed your distress sooner, I might not have acted like such a jackass over my own condition."

She touched his mouth with trembling fingers. "I meant what I said, Vince. You're very strong. I couldn't cope with blindness."

He caught her hand and held it in place for a moment, warming his lips. "I have a feeling you could cope with anything, Tiger." Then he released her fingers and brought her head back to his shoulder. Her sweet sigh soothed, diminished, the ache within him. But another ache was developing, one that was an exquisite torture.

Every time she shifted on his lap he had to bite his tongue to keep from moaning aloud. But he wouldn't have moved her for the world.

The sound of another car on the gravel driveway disturbed them. He tightened his arms briefly, then looped a strand of hair around his finger and tugged gently. "That's May's car." He chuckled into her ear. "It's getting harder and harder to carry on a seduction around here," he groused.

His offhand remark immobilized her for a brief moment. "Is that what this is?" she asked finally.

Her words brought a ghost of a smile to his face. "I must have lost my touch. Couldn't you tell?" he asked as he caressed her cheek with the back of his fingers.

She sat perfectly still waiting for more. May wouldn't mind.

At last, Vince dropped his hand and slipped his glasses back on. His manner was not as casual, however, as his words. This was not the cocky, sexy Vince of the past, sure of his appeal—this was instead a man bothered by uncertainty.

He assisted A.J. as she got to her feet. "You can always try again," she said lightly.

"I intend to."

She decided she'd best ignore that last remark, as she straightened her shirt. She didn't have time to do anything with her hair. She gave it a twist and brought it forward over her shoulder. "I wonder what May wants."

"I gave her a list of some things to get in town," he said.

She splashed her face at the sink in the mudroom before she went to the back door. "Hi, May. Wait, I'll help you." She propped open the door and hurried outside. The dog followed, greeting May like an old friend.

"You've been crying," May accused as soon as she saw A.J.

NO RISK, NO OBLIGATION TO BUY...NOW OR EVER!

CASINO JUBILEE
"Scratch'n Match" Game

Here's how to play:

1. Peel off label from front cover. Place it in space provided at right. With a coin, carefully scratch off the silver box. This makes you eligible to receive two or more free books, and possibly another gift, depending upon what is revealed beneath the scratch-off area.

2. Send back this card and you'll receive brand-new Silhouette Intimate Moments® novels. These books have a cover price of $3.50 each, but they are yours to keep absolutely free.

3. There's no catch. You're under no obligation to buy anything. We charge nothing – ZERO – for your first shipment. And you don't have to make any minimum number of purchases – not even one!

4. The fact is, thousands of readers enjoy receiving books by mail from the Silhouette Reader Service™ months before they're available in stores. They like the convenience of home delivery and they love our discount prices!

5. We hope that after receiving your free books you'll want to remain a subscriber. But the choice is yours – to continue or cancel, anytime at all! So why not take us up on our invitation, with no risk of any kind. You'll be glad you did!

YOURS FREE!

This lovely Victorian pewter-finish miniature is perfect for displaying a treasured photograph – and it's yours absolutely free – when you accept our no-risk offer.

© 1991 HARLEQUIN ENTERPRISES LIMITED

CASINO JUBILEE
"Scratch'n Match" Game

SCRATCH HERE

PLACE LABEL HERE

?

**CHECK CLAIM CHART BELOW
FOR YOUR FREE GIFTS!**

Name _____

Address _____ Apt. _____

City _____ State _____ Zip _____

▼ DETACH AND MAIL CARD TODAY! ▼

CASINO JUBILEE CLAIM CHART	
🍒🍒🍒	WORTH 4 FREE BOOKS AND A FREE VICTORIAN PICTURE FRAME
🍒🔔🍒	WORTH 4 FREE BOOKS
🔔🔔🍒	WORTH 3 FREE BOOKS

CLAIM N° 1528

THE SILHOUETTE READER SERVICE™ : HERE'S HOW IT WORKS

Accepting free books puts you under no obligation to buy anything. You may keep the books and gift and return the shipping statement marked "cancel." If you do not cancel, about a month later we will send you 6 additional novels and bill you just $2.71 each plus 25¢ delivery and applicable sales tax, if any.* That's the complete price, and – compared to cover prices of $3.50 each – quite a bargain! You may cancel at any time, but if you choose to continue, every month we'll send you 6 more books, which you may either purchase at the discount price... or return at our expense and cancel your subscription.

*Terms and prices subject to change without notice. Sales tax applicable in N.Y.

If offer card is missing, write to: Silhouette Reader Service, 3010 Walden Ave., P.O. Box 1867, Buffalo, NY 14269-1867

BUSINESS REPLY MAIL

FIRST CLASS MAIL   PERMIT NO. 717   BUFFALO, NY

POSTAGE WILL BE PAID BY ADDRESSEE

SILHOUETTE READER SERVICE
3010 WALDEN AVE
PO BOX 1867
BUFFALO NY 14240-9952

NO POSTAGE
NECESSARY
IF MAILED
IN THE
UNITED STATES

A.J. took a sack of groceries from the hatchback of May's small car. She straightened with the bag in her arms and smiled. "It was one of those therapeutic cries. I needed it."

May still looked worried. "Are you sure you're all right?"

"I'm sure. I feel better than I've felt in months." She led the way into the house.

"It seems so silly to have you do the shopping for us, when I have a car right here." She raised her voice, so he could hear, and earned herself a peculiar look from May.

"I can hear you," he said loudly from the main room. Then he laughed.

"He doesn't like for anyone to whisper about him," Amanda explained.

"I understand—I wouldn't like it, either." May had stopped for pizza on the way home, she told A.J. as they headed for the kitchen. "They were having a two-for-one sale. I hope you both like pepperoni pizza."

Vince followed them into the room. "Only if you'll stay and eat yours with us," he said, smiling. He put one arm across A.J.'s shoulders.

May observed all this with a keen eye. "I intend to. Why do you think I brought my own inside?" she asked lightly. "Let me finish putting the groceries away."

"I'll pour the drinks. Beer?"

"With pizza? Of course," May said.

"Amanda?" He took a pilsner glass from the cabinet and hesitated, waiting for her answer. She was taking napkins and place mats from the drawer.

"Beer's fine," she agreed. He took down another glass. Then he took two cold cans of beer and the milk carton from the refrigerator.

A.J. had seen him pour liquids before, but it never ceased to amaze her that he could fill a glass or cup to exactly the right level and not spill a single drop.

"It's a piece of cake," he had explained when she had asked about it. "When you can't see, you listen. The sound liquid makes when it's poured into a container changes tone as it rises toward the rim."

She had closed her eyes and listened and she understood. Now she wanted to see what he would do with a beer when it was foam rising toward the rim.

He opened the carton and filled his milk glass. "You can pour your own beer," he said with a trace of the old devilish grin, as though he'd read her mind.

There were only two stools at the pass-through counter, so A.J. opened one side of a drop-leaf side table and pulled up three chairs.

"You seem to be in an unusually good mood, Vince," May said when they were halfway through the pizza.

Vince grew thoughtful but eventually a smile softened his rugged features. Beneath the table his toe nudged the side of A.J.'s foot. "You might say I'm learning to count my blessings, May."

"Good for you," she told him, catching a string of cheese with her finger. She glanced at A.J., who avoided her gaze. "There's something so…therapeutic about counting your blessings. Did you tell A.J. that you accepted my dinner invitation?"

"No, I hadn't gotten around to it."

Later, A.J. and Vince stood at the door, in the fading afternoon sunlight, saying goodbye to May. When the car had disappeared, A.J. turned to him. "Let's take the dog for a walk," she urged.

Vince hesitated and she held her breath. "All right," he said with a half smile. "We'd both better get jackets. It's getting colder."

Sawdust was ecstatic to have both of them walk with him. He tugged on the leash, which Vince held, and they speeded up their steps.

A.J. tucked her hand through his arm and shivered. "You were right. It is getting colder."

Vince liked the feel of her against him. He tightened his arm. "Is it dark?" He couldn't believe he'd asked. He avoided asking for information if he could possibly help it. Hell, he could have checked his watch.

"It's dusky," she told him. "But there's plenty of light to see where we're going." She paused and inhaled the clean air. "This is really a beautiful spot. Now that the leaves have begun to change, it's spectacular. Across the lake from the cabin is a copse of trees that's reflected in the water. The pines are still green, of course, but the others are predominantly gold. I see some dark red, too, the color of burgundy. Those would be dogwoods, I think. I imagine it's pretty in the spring. The mountain peaks in the distance are purple."

They strode briskly along. *I didn't ask for a travelogue,* Vince thought, but he didn't say anything. It was his own fault, and the reason he never asked questions unnecessarily.

Even well-meaning friends thought they had to describe every setting in minute detail. It never occurred to them that you might not give a damn—that their descriptions brought regret and grief rather than appreciation.

Without warning, the surface beneath Vince's left foot sank a few inches and shifted from firm to soft. He lost his balance and had to put a hand to the ground to keep from falling flat on his face and taking Amanda with him. "Damn," he muttered, straightening. He felt awkward as he tried to resume walking, and he faltered again, with one foot higher than the other.

Without saying anything, Amanda increased the pressure of her hand on his arm. She steered him toward the right, back onto the path. He felt like a fool. Logically he knew it was a foolish way to feel.

But to stumble like someone with two left feet—and in front of Amanda...

Suddenly the good mood that had lightened the afternoon was gone. He wanted to shout his anger, bellow his fury to the skies. He itched to plant his fist in something unforgivably hard, like a tree or a boulder, to relieve his frustration. He wanted to kick the damned dog.

He wanted to cry.

He concentrated on staying on the path and was silent for the rest of the walk. When they returned to the cabin, he said a terse good-night and headed upstairs.

He didn't touch the weight machine. He didn't even think about it.

Chapter 6

A.J. expected Vince to call off the dinner with May. All day Tuesday he'd been in the detached, self-protective facade he'd worn when she'd first arrived.

But when May came by Wednesday morning, he surprised them both. "What time do you want us to be at your house?" he asked.

"Seven," May answered, glancing at A.J. delightedly.

A.J. shrugged. She hadn't told May about the walk around the lake, or Vince's stumbling, or his retreat into isolation afterward. But the older woman wasn't stupid; she could see from Vince's withdrawn attitude that something had happened.

"We'll be there," he said.

At ten before seven that evening, A.J. was giving her twist a last tuck when she heard Vince on the stairs. She fitted gold earrings into her lobes and checked her hem in the full-length mirror. The outfit was a favorite of hers; the silk blouse and matching skirt, belted in the same color, gave the look of a shirtwaist dress.

She picked up her purse and her coat and started to leave the room. Then she stopped, put them down again and went back to the dresser. Her mother had sent a new perfume for her birthday, and she hadn't even opened it. She rarely wore scent but tonight she misted herself in its spicy fragrance.

Her steps slowed as she glanced down into the room below and caught sight of him standing at the foot of the steps waiting for her.

He heard the tap of her heels and looked up. "Ready to go?" he asked politely.

"Yes," she answered breathlessly as she gaped at him.

He wore a dark gray suit, precisely tailored to the width of his shoulders. His shirt was white, his silk tie, crimson with navy stripes, arranged in a perfectly centered, strict Windsor knot. His black shoes were polished to a glossy shine, while his hair was combed neatly to one side from a sleek part.

His suit jacket was unbuttoned and pushed back on one side. That hand was in his pocket. The other arm was propped casually on the newel post. He looked . . . easy and comfortable in his body. He looked like the old Vince, the gifted, clever, confident man she'd known so long ago.

"You look magnificent, Vince," she said softly.

He blushed. He actually *blushed*—and dipped his chin briefly. "No nicks or cuts or shaving cream on my jaw?" he asked.

She shook her head as she halted on the step above him, grateful for once that he couldn't see her giddy smile. She dropped her coat over the stair rail as she chastised herself for acting like a silly rock groupie. Anyone would think she'd never seen a man in a suit before. A gorgeous man in a suit, she amended.

"No shaving cream," she assured him. "Do you realize this is the first time I've ever seen you without your uniform?" Her senses were stunned by the sandalwood scent of his after-shave. Her voice sounded rushed and whispery, confusing her.

His raised brow was accompanied by a half smile.

"I mean dressed up."

The smile grew to a grin.

"I mean..." Good Lord, what was wrong with her? "In a tie and all."

"I know what you mean." He held out his hand and she put hers into it. "You have an advantage over me. Tell me what you're wearing."

"A blue skirt and blouse with a belt."

The hand holding hers moved, following her arm until his fingers found her loose, wrist-length sleeve. He fingered the fabric. "Blue silk." He held her upper arm in a light grasp, making a warm bracelet on her skin. "Is the dress the color of your eyes?"

She swallowed, had to think a minute. "It's almost the same color."

"Then it's sapphire blue, the color of the Pacific in deep water near Hawaii. I already know you're wearing high heels and new perfume. Jewelry?"

"Gold earrings."

He touched her lobes, found the small loops there. "No rings, bracelet?"

"No. I'm not in the habit of wearing much jewelry. It gets in the way when I'm working."

His hand curved around her nape; his thumb found the pulse in her neck. "Your hair's up."

"Yes." She waited for him to criticize her choice. Instead he laughed under his breath. "I'll bet you look elegant. And untouchable."

Vince gave himself a mental shake. "Let's go." He headed her toward the carport door. He didn't hesitate on the steps or when they reached the car. He circled the vehicle and got in on the passenger side. He could feel Amanda watching his movements. Her steps faltered, but she didn't question his adroitness.

She also didn't know that he'd gotten up at the crack of dawn yesterday and this morning to practice, memorizing the height of the steps, the distance to the car, the location of the door handle, until he was perfect. He'd be damned if he was going to make a fool of himself in front of her again.

"It's still early. How about a fire?" asked Vince when they returned to the cabin three hours later.

"That would be nice," said A.J. She kicked off her heels and settled on the sofa facing the hearth.

The dinner party had gone without a hitch. They'd toured May's house when they'd first arrived.

Vince had been appreciative, asking for details. Pleased, May had given them, then gone on to describe the architectural features and, during the meal, had told them several amusing historical anecdotes about the house and her extensive family.

The main course had been fresh grilled mountain brook trout, which was delicious. All in all it had been a most enjoyable evening.

So why couldn't she relax?

Vince took off his jacket and rolled his sleeves back to his elbows. His tie hung at a lopsided angle and the top button of his shirt was undone. The tinted glasses were in place, endowing him with a hint of mystery.

A.J. noted the care with which he built the fire in the large stone fireplace. He stacked the logs in the far back of the opening so there was no danger of their rolling out. He was careful to replace the screen as soon as he'd lit the kindling.

He joined her on the sofa, and they propped their stockinged feet on the coffee table in front of them. The initial flames were small, ineffectual licks against the logs. But the fire was noisy, spitting and crackling like fighting kittens. A.J. watched its gutsy efforts to devour something ten times larger than it was.

"May's dinner was delicious, wasn't it? I wonder where she gets the trout," said Vince casually.

"I'll ask her," A.J. replied. She rested her head against the back of the sofa and stared into the fire. "Vince, will you tell me what happened Monday evening?" she asked after a moment. She hated to bring up the subject, but she needed an answer if she was to avoid a repetition of whatever it was that set him off. "Did I do something wrong?"

"No," Vince answered without hesitation. "It wasn't you. It was me." He sighed, took his tie off and folded it with deliberate care, giving himself time to think. "I know I owe you an apology," he said as he laid the folded silk aside. His expression was somber.

"I don't need an apology, but I do need—or want—to understand. Was it because I gave you a hand up when you stumbled? Was I supposed to let you flounder?"

"Every now and then I—" He stopped. When he resumed, his voice had dropped an octave, the only outward sign of emotion he would allow himself. "I can't say I forget that I'm blind because I don't ever forget. But sometimes I forget that I can't do exactly what I want to do. I guess I get too sure of myself. When that happens I blunder, like I did that night when I stepped off the path and fell—and I'm immediately reminded of who and what I am."

He reached for her hand and clasped it lightly on the sofa between them. "The reminder isn't gentle," he went on cynically. "It's more like a flood of regret that overwhelms me. My mood turns black. I know I should fight against the melancholy, but I haven't learned how yet.

"And now, Dr. Upton," he said, deliberately lightening his tone, "you know more about my blind soul than any of the air force psychologists I've talked to."

She turned her head and looked at him. "Your blind *soul?*"

"Yeah. Or ego, persona, spirit, whatever." He lifted their clasped hands onto his thigh and ran his fingers across her knuckles. Her skin was as soft as a kitten's belly. "I know it sounds melodramatic, but I feel like my whole identity has changed."

"Well…everyone goes through periods of change— 'passages,' someone once called them. Maybe that's what's happening to you."

He was puzzled. "What do you mean?"

A.J. studied the growing flames, smelled the woodsmoke and tried to phrase her answer carefully. "Things always came easy for you. You were the golden boy—brilliant, talented, athletic. I remember my father saying you had everything going for you." She smiled and the smile was reflected in her voice when she teased, "Maybe you didn't understand how it was for us lesser mortals. Maybe this is an opportunity for you to learn."

She fully expected him to protest. But as he had this morning, he surprised her. "I can't take credit for any of that. I was lucky, that's all. And maybe you're right. Maybe I needed taking down a peg to learn a few things," he said thoughtfully.

A comfortable silence followed. She felt relaxed and drowsy. "The first fire of the season makes me sad," she said at last.

Vince's hand squeezed hers. "I like the first fire," he said.

"Not me. Long months of cold weather before spring comes again? Autumn isn't so bad, but winter is bleak."

Vince pulled her closer, slid his arm around her shoulders and fitted her to his side. She felt the heat of his hard chest beneath her breast. "Hey, Doc, let's be optimistic here," he commanded gruffly. "The first fire can also signal long months of cuddling to keep warm."

At his words, the drowsy tone of her mood quickened sharply. She laughed, trying to maintain a casual atmosphere, when in reality she was thrilled by the response. Here again was the old Vince Thornborough. Here again was the upbeat, positive man she'd known in the past. He was better. He was definitely better.

The telephone rang. Vince held her when she would have gotten up. He reached out for the cordless receiver on the table beside him.

But when he said, "John, how are you?" she displaced his arm and shifted slightly away from him.

"Just a minute, I'll ask her. Your father wants to know if you have plans for Saturday. He would like to come up and spend the night." His furrowed brow indicated that he was surprised.

"He's *asking?*" she whispered in mock amazement.

Vince grinned and squeezed her thigh.

Then she spoke in a normal voice. "Fine. I have no plans until the first of next week."

"Sure, John." Vince listened for a minute. "Of course, I'll ask her. See you tomorrow afternoon."

He hung up. "Well, well," he said, a grin forming on his lips. "He wants us to invite May over for dinner. He'll bring the steaks and wine."

She told him about her own speculation about May and her father. "She's so different from the other women he's dated."

"Maybe he'll continue to see her when he retires next year. Retirement will be a big adjustment for John. He's accustomed to being surrounded by people every day. She could help him get past that."

"It's always been his choice to live that way," A.J. answered, suddenly defensive. "I'm sure any number of women would have been happy to fill the gaps in his life. But he would never marry any of them."

Vince was silent for a minute, and then he reached for her hand again. "Amanda, I wonder if you ever realized how much your father loved your mother, how devastated he was when she left him. I wasn't around then, of course, but I've heard the stories. He apparently went kind of crazy for a while. He blamed himself for the breakup."

She laughed bitterly and pulled her hand from his. She linked her fingers in her lap. "Mother says the blame is hers. She couldn't stand the isolation when he was gone, the worry or the loneliness. She used to say they were two nice people who should never have gotten involved with each other." And that should be a warning for you, she told herself, edging a bit farther away from him. Vince was far too much like her father.

"I don't think any woman he's dated since has ever lived up to her."

"Look who he dates." She spread her hands. "Career women who don't want marriage, women who are inappropriately young—he never dates anyone he might build a relationship with."

"Until now," Vince agreed. "But you just made my point. He didn't think he would ever get over your mother, and he says you look very much like her."

A.J. stared at his face painted gold by the firelight. She was stunned by his words. "Oh, no, I look nothing at all like my mother."

"To him you do. You always have. He told me one time that you were the image of her."

A.J. looked back at the flames, her heart pounding uncomfortably in her chest. "Our hair's the same," she said thoughtfully. "And we both have blue eyes."

She swallowed an uncomfortable lump in her throat. "I never knew he thought so. All these years—I thought my father was just doing his duty when he had me visit, that he really couldn't stand me."

"Not that—never that," Vince said quietly. "He isn't an easy man to understand."

She was silent for a long time, recalling May's comment that John was proud of her. She'd dismissed it, but now she wondered if he simply had difficulty expressing himself. Then she released a shuddering sigh. "I wish I had known this when I was younger," she said in a soft, sorry voice. "It might have made it easier. My visits seemed like endurance contests, and I was so hurt. But I might have understood if I'd known."

"It's never too late to mend fences, Tiger," Vince said quietly.

"I'm glad you said that, Vince." A.J. sat forward and wrapped her arms around her knees. "I hope this time you'll let me get it all said and mend ours." She combed escaping wisps of hair away from her face, took a deep breath and faced him. "I'm genuinely sorry for what I did. I look back, and I'm unable to believe I was so callous."

"Amanda, I told you, this isn't necessary."

"It is for me. Please let me say it all, then I won't mention it again."

"Okay."

She didn't let his heavy sigh or his less-than-enthusiastic permission deter her. "I'm sure it's no surprise that I was wildly in love with you when I was sixteen. Heck, I was in love with you when I was fourteen. A silly, teenage crush, of course, but at the time the feelings were very real to me. That night…oh God, that awful night."

Her eyes fell to her lap as the memories came rushing in. She replayed the evening fourteen years ago as though it were yesterday, while she told him the whole story.

John had taken her to the officers' club for a luau. It was her last night in Hawaii, and her father was in remarkably good humor. The club was festively decorated; the show had been arranged by one of the best island clubs on Waikiki.

As had happened so many times in the past, halfway through the show, John was called away.

A.J. didn't try to hide her disappointment. She was leaving tomorrow and wouldn't see him for another year. She would have thought he'd make an extra effort to spend this last night with her. "I don't want to go yet," she told him airily, "but I'll find a ride. Don't worry about me."

He finally gave in, but to her dismay, he asked Vince to see her home. Vince was probably the only young man on the base that John Upton trusted completely to look out for her. And John didn't know about the words they'd had.

Vince concealed his reluctance, giving her a smile as he agreed. After the show, she said goodbye to the people she'd met during her visit. She hinted that she and Vince had further plans for the evening.

She joined Vince in the parking lot. He was quiet as he held the door of his car for her. It was a short drive, but to A.J. it seemed to take forever as he gave one-word responses to all of her attempts to make conversation. She invited him in for coffee but he declined, saying that he had a date with one of the women in the show.

A.J. fought back the tears as she faced him and let her anger show. Why hadn't he simply told her father he had other plans? she demanded. At least it would have been honest.

Vince answered calmly that John was putting in a lot of hours, and he didn't need any more worries right now. If it would relieve John to know his daughter was delivered safely home, Vince would do so. Then he made his biggest mistake. He tried to lecture her again—this time about her father. Her wildness had been a concern to John all summer.

She erupted. What the hell did he know about her relationship with her father? He knew nothing of missed birthdays, broken schedules, planes not met, promises not kept. She'd been shaking when she'd slammed in through the front door of the house.

And called a taxi. She was going into Honolulu. She'd heard some others at the luau discussing a nightclub downtown. It was her last night in Hawaii and by God, she was going to enjoy it. She was in the mood to do something crazy, something reckless.

Ed Wilson was another of the pilots in her father's squadron. He was also the first person she'd seen when she walked into the dimly lit club. He recognized her immediately and became flatteringly attentive. She had to admit to herself that she was relieved.

The place was on the edge of a pretty rough section of town. The drinking was heavy. A.J. felt only a brief pang of conscience, then she threw herself into the spirit of the party. Sometime during the course of the evening she realized that Ed had dumped her and gone off with someone else. She knew a moment's qualm, then dismissed it.

The police raided the place at 4:00 a.m. and arrested the owners. She'd managed a phone call to Vince, but she'd gotten an answering machine.

By the time her father arrived at the juvenile detention hall, he was so angry he wouldn't speak to her.

They drove back to his quarters. She was grateful for his silence as she packed her clothes. If he had talked to her, she would have cried, and she didn't want anyone to see her in tears. Jail. God, she'd been in jail!

As he put her on the plane, however, he finally broke his silence. The edge had worn off his explosive temper and when he spoke he was calm. "How did you even know about that club, A.J.?"

Tears clogged her throat as she turned away from her father and entered the jetway. "Ask Vince," she tossed carelessly over her shoulder.

She hadn't known that Vince had been called on the carpet. She hadn't known that he'd been accused of taking an underage female, her, to the off-limits club.

The woman he'd had a date with had left on a show tour of the Far East. No one came forward to support his story that he had taken Amanda directly home, that he had never even been to that club.

A.J. first heard of the story when she received a phone call from Ed a week or so after she got back to Florida. He was tentative in his request that she not reveal his part in the evening. She listened in dismay as he described the questioning Vince had undergone. But he quickly reassured her. Vince had had a witness—the beautiful Eurasian showgirl with whom he'd had a date would be back on the island soon. He would be cleared of any wrongdoing over the incident.

But there would always be a smear on his reputation, she knew. She was aware of how the military worked. Even though he was innocent, it would take Vince a long time to live down the gossip.

When she questioned Ed as to why he didn't come forward to save his friend a lot of hassle, he said that Vince's reputation and his top-notch standing with her father could stand the black mark a lot better than his—Ed's—could.

Finally, after some deep soul-searching, A.J. mustered her courage and called John to admit that Vince had indeed delivered her home. From what she gathered, the damage had already been done. And she wouldn't give her father the names of the other people at the club.

She finished her story. "I was so mad at you. I know now that you were trying to make me face facts, but when you called me a spoiled brat and a pain in the ass, it really hurt."

"I didn't!" he protested.

"Oh, yes, you did," she retorted. Then her voice softened. "And you were right."

His smile was crooked. "Well, yeah," he drawled.

"Anyway, when we left the officers' club I had told people at the luau that you were taking me out. I had heard somebody mention a nightclub where some of the guys were going afterward. So, when you dropped me off, I called a taxi and went, too.

"That nightclub was awful, Vince. I got scared sometime during the evening. I tried to call you, to explain and ask you to help me. But no one answered, of course. When John showed up at the jail, he wouldn't even talk to me. The nightclub owner told him I'd been dancing with an officer. He assumed it was you, and I let him think that." Her voice grew thick with unshed tears. "I thought he wouldn't be mad if I was with you, that you couldn't do wrong in his eyes. But I quickly found out that I was mistaken. John didn't relent, did he, even for his fair-haired boy?"

"No, he didn't. Not until later, when the truth came out." He leaned forward and laid his hand on her back and began to massage gently.

She shrugged against the weight of his hand. "Don't. I don't deserve comforting, Vince," she said harshly. "I was—I still am—so ashamed."

"Amanda, you called and straightened everything out. You got off track for a while. But I want you to put it behind you."

"I've tried." She lifted her head and stared into the fire. The flames were blurred, but she didn't notice; she was looking into the past. "The night, after I talked to John, I went off by myself. I took a long look at myself, and I didn't like what I saw. I cried until there were no more tears left inside me. And I thought a lot. What was I to become? What was to become of me? I made a promise that night. To myself, and I guess to you, too, in a way."

"To me?"

She heard surprise in his voice, but she didn't turn to look. "Yes. You were the person I'd wronged. I promised that I'd do something with my life. That I wouldn't depend on anyone else to do it for me. That I would make a difference.''

Vince was deeply touched by her admission. "And you have been successful. I'm glad, Amanda," he said quietly. "Now, forget it. That's an order."

Her laughter was choked. "Okay, Major. I won't mention it again."

He pondered for a moment. "I do have one more question. Who was the other officer?"

"What?"

"The officer. The one you were dancing with."

She certainly wasn't going to tell him it was his good friend Ed Wilson. "Nobody important. I just wish I hadn't been such a brat. Maybe John would have liked me more if I—"

Vince interrupted. "Amanda, you promised—"

"Really, Vince, I'm all right now about my father. I've learned to live with it."

He traced a design across her back with his finger. "Is that enough? Learning to live with it? Wouldn't you rather be friends?"

"I don't know," she answered honestly. The flames were full-grown now, reaching upward into the dark chimney.

"Think about it, will you?"

She was silent for a minute. She'd heard several things during this conversation that she'd never expected to hear. She'd never known she reminded John of her mother. She'd never known he was so affected by the divorce. If that was true, she was surprised he'd even had her for summer visits. "I'll think about it," she agreed.

Vince sank back into the sofa cushions and linked his fingers over his stomach. "I wanted you, you know, all those years ago. Damn, you turned me on."

She was still thinking about her father. When his words finally registered, she whipped her head around. "What?"

He removed his tinted glasses and held them by one stem. He gave the glasses a spin, a casual move that was belied by the huskiness in his voice when he spoke again. "You grew up when I wasn't paying attention, Tiger."

"I made an impression, huh?"

"A lasting impression," he said in a dry tone. "From one summer to the next, you suddenly looked fantastic in your tennis whites and sensational in a bikini. It was tough on my libido, but I liked you too much to do something stupid. Besides, I knew your father would have my hide if I touched you. You might not have looked too young, but you were."

A.J. was deeply touched by his confession and oddly reassured. They *had* been good friends, and he'd cared about her. She dug for her sense of humor and felt a smile grow. "Vince Thornborough was turned on by me?" she said softly, wonderingly. "If I'd known that, *no* one would have been able to stand me."

Vince chuckled and tugged at the back of her shirt, freeing it from the belt and waistband of her skirt. "Well, you know now," he said softly as his hand slid over her bare skin. He circled her midriff until his warm fingers rested under her breast.

A.J.'s heart took the now-familiar leap.

"And you're all grown-up. And though I can't see you, my memory is very, very good." He laid the glasses aside. Then his other arm came around her and he pulled her back against his chest.

She rested there for a minute.

"I remember your deep blue eyes. I remember your bare shoulders, honey warm from the sun, and smooth, so smooth. Your breasts were full and high. And your soft, pretty thighs." He sighed. "Oh, yeah, I remember your thighs."

A.J.'s body grew slack against his shoulder. Her head swam dizzily; her thoughts were incoherent. She shivered, once, when his fingers brushed her nipple, then withdrew. She ached to take his big hand in hers, to place it over her breast, but there was a reason why she shouldn't. She couldn't quite pinpoint the reason, but it was there, like a distant figure, unidentifiable but tangible.

Her memories of him were equally vivid—memories of his broad, tanned shoulders, his strong, muscular legs and arms, dusted with dark hair. She shook her head in an effort to clear it. "Vince..."

Moving with a greater urgency than he'd shown before, he nuzzled her neck, seeking the exquisitely tender place below her ear.

She felt his tongue touch her skin and nearly melted at the sensation. "Vince." Was that her voice, that husky, sensual purr? She laid her hands on his crossed arms, not disengaging them, but not returning the embrace, either. "Is this a good idea?"

"I don't know." He lifted his head, pondering for a moment. His eyes were closed and there was a half smile on his lips. "It feels good."

She turned within his arms and flattened her palms against his chest. The texture of his shirt was crisp beneath her fingers. She fought the temptation to lay her cheek against the cool, starched cotton. "It feels too good," she protested weakly. "We have to stop."

Vince bent his head to capture her lips. They parted for him. She tilted her head back and her tongue joined his, tasting, exploring. The kiss was long and deep and ignited sparks of longing.

She was not only on fire, she was alive and eager and hungry. She wanted to succumb to these glorious sensations, more than she'd ever wanted anything. But she dared not.

Her head was spinning so; she still didn't remember why she needed to stop. She clung to her reason by a thread, but she clung.

At last he sighed heavily and dropped his hands. "Something's wrong, isn't it? I want you, Amanda," he said. "Does that worry you?"

"Yes," she answered, gathering her composure, searching for balance, sitting up straight, but with effort. "Actually, it scares me to death because I want you, too. But I'm not the type to hop into bed just to satisfy the first twinges of desire, Vince."

"Hell, neither am I." He found his glasses and replaced them. "But I've just admitted that I wanted you back then. So these twinges are hardly the first for either of us."

No, we've been waiting for fourteen years. The emotion she was feeling now wasn't the eternal love she'd thought she had felt at sixteen, but this hunger, this desire, was definitely a more powerful, more compelling emotion.

A voice from within her demanded, "Are you going to wait another fourteen years before you have what you've always wanted?"

She had no reply.

A.J. found herself standing in the hallway, looking out a window awaiting her father's arrival. She was dressed conservatively, in chestnut woolen slacks and an ecru silk blouse. Her hair was freshly washed and arranged in her typical, no-nonsense style and her makeup had been carefully applied. Her shoes had medium heels. She wanted to look efficient, well-groomed, in order to heighten her own self-confidence.

Should she decide to take Vince's advice and put out feelers toward a closer relationship with John, she sure wouldn't begin from a position of inadequacy. And she would have to be very cautious. John had talked to Vince about his feelings for her mother, but he'd spoken in confidence.

Vince. Her pulse accelerated at the thought of him. She had wanted to make love with him last night. He'd held her caringly, he'd kissed her—she'd never been so intoxicated by a man's kisses.

But she'd pulled away. For the rest of the night she'd tossed in her bed, thinking about Vince's yen for her all those years ago, and relishing his current desire.

However, this wasn't the right time; maybe there would never be a right time. She had a job to do. It was more important for him to heal, to rebuild. If they became involved romantically, she wouldn't be able to help him as she longed to.

A red Jeep appeared in the driveway. She watched curiously, wondering who it belonged to, as it rolled to a stop. Her father stepped out of the vehicle.

She hurried along to the mudroom and met him at the back door. He was dressed in freshly pressed chinos and a parka and carried a bottle of red wine and a package wrapped in butcher's paper. As always he looked more approachable in civies. "You have a new car," she said, holding the door open for him.

He nodded and kissed her temple as was his habit. She wished just one time he would hug her.

"How do you like it?" he asked, looking back at the vehicle fondly.

"I like it. But—" She didn't complete the thought.

"I know," he interrupted with a brief smile. "It isn't my normal conservative sedan, is it? But I needed to trade, and I'm thinking ahead to next year. When I retire I might need a four-wheel drive."

A bright red one? she thought, but she didn't say it aloud. "Especially if you don't have your driveway repaired." She returned his smile and took the wine and package he held out to her.

Suddenly his brows shot up. "What's this?"

She hadn't realized that the dog had been standing beside her. He left her side to sniff at John's trousers. "This is Dusty—short for Sawdust. My dog."

He scowled. "I hope he doesn't have fleas."

"He has a flea collar," she said emotionlessly.

Before they entered the main room, he stopped her with a hand on her arm. "How is Vince?" he asked in a lowered voice.

"He's gained some weight since I got here," she answered, her tone at a normal pitch. She ignored his frown. "And I can testify as to the excellent condition of his temper, because I've been on the receiving end of it. I whispered to someone about him when he couldn't hear. He really hates that."

John gave her a sharp look and led the way into the main room.

Vince turned from the fireplace. "Did you get the message, John?" he asked.

"I think I got the message," John answered. "You don't like for people to discuss you out of your hearing." He crossed to shake the younger man's outstretched hand, then he stepped back for a look. "You have gained some weight. You look better."

"Ah, well, I have my own private chef," Vince said, settling back in one corner of the sofa. He grinned as A.J., who had detoured to the kitchen to put down her father's offerings, returned to the room. "And she's a damned good one, too."

She joined the circle, sitting in the other corner of the sofa, and listened to their small talk. John stood with his back to the fire, hands linked behind him, looking down at them. She thought, not for the first time, how alike the two men were.

After a few minutes, the small talk trailed off. John didn't speak for a minute; he seemed to be speculating. "A.J. is acting chef? I thought she was a doctor," he said ponderously.

A.J. could feel his disapproval. He'd sent her here to do one job, and she was doing another one. His interpretation irritated her. What he didn't see was that if you "feed the body, you feed the soul." She was trying to face this problem creatively, and he could only see it in a straightforward way.

What she didn't know was that Vince was also irritated by John's attitude. It had been years since he'd been with father and daughter in the same room, and this time his sympathies lay with Amanda. Though he couldn't see, he could certainly sense the tension between them. He'd forgotten how stiff and unbending John was when he was near her. He wasn't that way with anyone else. Damn the man—he was a friend, a good friend—but he did have a blind spot where his daughter was concerned.

A.J. caught Vince's smile and was puzzled. It was not a smile of amusement.

"But Amanda isn't here as a doctor. She's looking for a job, and this is her base of operations," he said smoothly, very smoothly. "Right, John?"

Gotcha, thought A.J. John was well and truly caught. He had the grace to look away from her.

She wanted to laugh, but she held herself to a smile. "I'm on vacation from being a doctor," she said quickly, and got to her feet again. "As a matter of fact, I should get started on our dinner."

"What time is May coming?" Vince asked when she'd gone into the kitchen.

"I'm picking her up at six-thirty," John said. "I'll leave in a few minutes." He sat in the corner of the sofa that A.J. had vacated. "Are you really making progress?"

"Depends on what you mean," Vince answered pensively. "There's no change in my vision."

"You'd better hope not. You couldn't hope to pass your review now, even if your vision were perfect."

"What do you mean by that?" Vince demanded sharply. He got to his feet. Frowning, he shoved his hands into the pockets of his slacks and rocked slightly on his heels. "You make me sound like a deadbeat."

John was up to something. If he could see, he could tell by the older man's expression what that was.

"We both know you're no deadbeat." John hesitated. "But if your eyesight was restored a hundred percent tomorrow, you couldn't return to the flight line or even to active duty, Vince. You're fooling yourself if you think you could. You've lost tensile strength along with your lost weight, and I'd be willing to bet your reflexes are way off."

Vince inhaled sharply, unmollified by the explanation because it was the truth, and the truth hurt like hell. He clenched his jaw. His pitiful attempts on the weight-building apparatus in his room attested to that.

He stifled a violent urge within himself to lash out and was quiet for a long time. "You're playing hardball today, aren't you?" he said finally.

"Or you're extra touchy."

Vince combed his hair back with his fingers. His hand remained at the back of his neck to massage the tension there. "Yeah, maybe I am."

John glanced at his watch and got to his feet. "It's almost six-thirty. May will be waiting. Would you like to take a ride in my new car?"

"No, you go ahead. I'll stay here and help Amanda."

John took his keys out of his pocket. He hesitated, jingling them absently in his palm. "You still call her Amanda?"

"Yeah. It's a pretty name. I don't know why you'd shorten it. Were you trying to make her into a boy?"

"Hell, no," John answered with honest horror in his tone. Then he lowered his head and shrugged. "I don't remember how it started."

John left, and Vince joined A.J. in the kitchen.

"Thank you," she said. She was rubbing the baking potatoes with vegetable oil.

"For what?"

"For saying I have a pretty name."

"You're welcome."

Her voice was stern when she went on. "Just don't try to get me to call him 'Daddy.'"

Vince gave a hoot of laughter. "Never. What can I do?"

"You can wash and chop the vegetables. They're in the sink."

He went to the sink and turned on the water; she stowed the potatoes in the microwave oven. "John got a new car?" he asked after a minute.

"A Jeep, a red one."

"I don't believe it," he said. A look of amazement crossed his face. "Red? You think he's going through some kind of mid-life crisis?"

"John?" she sniffed. She jabbed a few buttons and the oven came to life. "John Upton's been in a mid-life crisis since he was old enough to vote."

He selected a knife from the holder and began to chop the mushrooms. "You heard everything he said?"

"About your condition? Yes."

"Maybe I should hear more about the training plan you mentioned."

He was surprised when she pinched his arm. "So you'll do it because he says to?" she demanded.

"Ouch. A doctor should know better than to torment a disabled man," he protested, but he was grinning. "No, I'll do it because I want to fly again."

She hugged him from behind.

John left early the next morning.

A.J. had realized after seeing them together that her father was serious about May and she about him. They exchanged looks of such warmth and awareness that A.J. found herself envious. She wondered if she would ever experience such intimacy, such personal communication that no words were needed.

John's personality, even his appearance, underwent a total modification in the presence of the older woman. His stern countenance became an indulgent smile; the rigid shoulders relaxed into a position of easy comfort; and his eyes, which could be so cold and expressionless, were warm and accepting.

Still, she hoped the other woman knew what she was getting into.

Though occasional tension could be felt in the atmosphere between herself and her father, their conversations flowed fairly smoothly. With May's influence, and Vince's, a relationship with her father might be possible.

May had reopened the subject of A.J.'s search for a hospital. Again she had suggested an interview with the local facility.

A.J. had quickly looked to her father to judge his reaction.

He had frowned.

Chapter 7

On Monday, midmorning, A.J. left to visit a hospital that was only an hour's drive away.

The trip took up the rest of the day. She met other doctors in the small town, had lunch with the hospital administrator, learned a few unpleasant things and toured the town.

When she returned to the cabin that evening, Vince had dinner started. "It smells delicious," she said as she stepped out of her high heels. She was distracted.

"Your soup from the freezer, but my cornbread," he said. He took the pan of bread from the oven and turned his head in her direction. "You want to tell me what's wrong? I take it you didn't like the town?"

She wasn't surprised that he'd picked up on her annoyance. "It wasn't the town so much." She began to wander the room, her stocking-clad feet making no noise on the tiled floor.

"The people?"

"The people, most of them, were nice but I *hated* the hospital."

When she didn't explain or continue, he prodded her. "Was it underequipped? Unsanitary? Too small or too big? What?"

"None of the above. The local hospital I visited today has to answer to a corporate office somewhere else," she said, almost to herself.

"I'm not sure I understand."

"I've heard of them, of course. They're the latest trend in medicine," she explained as she started to pace. "The institutions are run like a chain of motels. And the spin doctors—the public-relations experts they hire to sell the idea—have a great pitch. They're efficient, cost effective..." She began to pace. "If you don't care that someone in a corporate office a thousand miles away is making the decisions about your community's health care, fine. I can see all the advantages, but I don't think I would like to practice medicine that way. They're just too slick."

She stopped pacing a step from where he stood. "What the people in these communities don't realize, until it's too late, is that they also lose local control over their systems. If they don't like what's going on, that's tough. This hospital I visited today charges six dollars for an aspirin. Six dollars for a drug that may cost a nickel retail." Her voice rose with her indignation.

Vince was leaning, one hip against the counter, with his arms folded across his chest. At the sight of his grin, her shoulders slumped. "I know, I'm overreacting. But I want to live in a town that has made a commitment to its own good health, not turned it over to someone else for convenience' sake."

"You don't hear me arguing, do you? I think you have a lot of heart."

"You do?" she asked softly.

He nodded and reached for her. She went willingly into his arms. She felt secure, comforted. It was not a feeling she was accustomed to, but she liked it.

"I can understand your conviction," he said across the top of her head. "City Hospital is county owned, isn't it?"

"Yes." She nodded against his chest. "And, I'll admit, they're always short of money and the paperwork drives them crazy. But they work for, and answer to, the people in the Atlanta area, not a corporation somewhere."

"So? Eliminate all the corporations from your consideration."

"I plan to. I just hope there are a few places left."

He kissed the top of her head and released her. "The cornbread's getting cold. Your mail's on the counter. Have a seat, and I'll serve."

She was amazed at how reluctant she was to move out of his arms. "Okay," she said with a sigh.

Vince carefully ladled the steaming soup into man-size bowls. While he set the dishes on the pass-through counter, she read her mail, only occasionally glancing at him. She was no longer concerned about his burning himself, or cutting himself. He was adept and capable in the kitchen. And everywhere else, for that matter.

The mail included two more inquiries about the résumés she'd sent out. She dug in her purse for her calendar and made a face when she looked at next week's schedule. The long trip, when she would visit several hospitals and be gone overnight, was coming up soon, as well.

She was anxious to get Vince well established in his training routine before she left. They had worked out a schedule, and he had exercised yesterday and this morning. By her evaluation he was amazingly sound for all he'd been through. The first night, when he'd immobilized her at the back door, should have taught her that.

He rounded the counter and sat beside her. His hand ran quickly across her back in a gesture of comfort. "Hey," he said calmly. "You'll find something."

"I know." She described her schedule. "I'm supposed to be on vacation," she groaned in mock despair.

Late the next afternoon an autumn sun beat down unmercifully on Vince's head. Despite temperatures in the fifties, sweat poured off him, wetting his hair and clothes, stinging his eyes, making his palms slick. He groaned aloud. The muscles in his shoulders bunched painfully. The ones in his calves were tied in knots.

"Come on, just a few more, and then you can quit." A.J. held a stopwatch over him.

Suddenly his arms gave way and he collapsed on the grass, fighting for breath. "No more," he gasped.

"You only did eighteen," she scolded. "Okay, that's one more than yesterday. Get up."

Instead of doing as she asked, he grabbed her ankle. He sat up even as she fell, and maneuvered her slender body so that she landed on his lap, facing him, her legs stretched out on either side of his hips.

She draped her arms across his shoulders, her hands dangling on his back. "Now I know why they call them sweat suits," she teased.

"Oh, yeah?" He slid his hands under her shirt and began to tickle.

"No, no. Vince! I'm sorry. I can't *stand* to be tickled."

But he had already forgotten about the tickling. Her skin felt like the softest silk. He brushed the heels of his hands against the outside curve of her breasts. Brushed again. Then he gave another, completely different kind of moan as his large hands covered her, squeezing her with a gentle but firm caress.

It was as though her flimsy bra didn't exist and, in a moment, it did not. He unhooked it and brought it and her shirt together over her head. Her nipples responded instantly to the cool air, and to his touch, tightening to stiff buds.

Vince felt energy that he hadn't felt since the crash. He was suddenly strong, indomitable—and desperate. She had taken to wearing her hair loose most of the time, fastened only with a piece of yarn or a barrette at her nape. He freed the dark mass now, spreading the strands across her shoulders like a cape. His desire was full-blown and he knew she was aware of it. His voice was a hoarse slur. "Oh, Amanda, stop me now or..."

"Vince," A.J. whispered. Her breathing grew shallow as he also whipped off his shirt. "We shouldn't. Somebody will see. And you've been exercising."

"Damn it. Turn off the doctor mode, Amanda. Just be a woman."

A woman? He wanted her to just be a woman. He was exploring every inch of her torso, the tactile sensations of his fingers making her want as she'd never wanted before. Yes, he made her feel very much a woman.

But this wasn't good for him; he should cool down. "Vince, you're hot."

"God, yes, I'm hot, I'm sizzling," he growled. Slowly he pulled her close until her nipples were buried, lost in the soft, curly hair on his chest. He moved her slightly, increasing the friction between their bodies. "I want you Amanda. I need this to happen," he muttered against her parted lips.

He'd said he wanted her before, and she'd thrown up a defensive wall around her own longing. This time she had no such urge to protect herself. She discovered suddenly that her desire was as potent as his, as uncontrollable. She was ready to make love with this man, ready on some primitive level to mate with him.

"Oh, yes," she said huskily, her voice echoing her hunger. "Yes, Vince. I need you, too."

She let go of all the checks, all the self-restraint that she'd cultivated over the years. All the carefully thought-out qualities and behavior that signaled maturity were gone on a puff of smoke. Suddenly she was sixteen again, with raging hormones—merely a living, breathing creature with an intense longing to ease an ache that had lasted for fourteen years.

All her misgivings disappeared. Years ago she had stored away her yearning for this man. But the intervening time had not dimmed the intensity of her feelings.

The heat between them would have melted an iceberg. She no longer noticed the chill in the air; she no longer thought about being outside, well within sight of the driveway. Instead she drove her fingers into his hair. Her tongue joined his in a wet impassioned dance of exploration. Instinctively she moved her hips against his hardness, seeking to be closer.

He broke off the kiss and arched her back over his arm, his mouth seeking her breast. "Oh, I wish I could see you."

The whispered statement brought her close to sanity again, close enough for her to realize that, with the temperature of the air and ground, this could get to be uncomfortable, close enough for her to say, "Let's go inside, Vince."

She wasn't sure how they made it. The dog greeted them curiously and jubilantly when they came in, but at a word from Vince, he slunk to the corner and left them alone. At last they were up the stairs and finally they were sprawled across his bed.

Vince made a visible effort to slow down as he stripped off her pants and sneakers and socks. Then he disposed of his own clothes and stood erect. His need was strong and full. The sunlight streaming through the window painted his splendid body a shining gold.

She touched him. Her fingers were cool on his body.

He inhaled quickly, sharply, then said her name as he came to her and took her in his arms again. He lay in the juncture of her thighs, propped on his elbows, his big body looming over her slight one. Brushing the hair off her face, he smiled, and she melted. "Do something for me, sweetheart," he murmured.

"Yes," she answered without hesitation. She would have agreed to anything at just this moment.

"Close your eyes."

She smiled, knowing what the request meant. "All right. They're closed."

"Now we're even," he breathed against her neck.

He smelled slightly of sweat and outdoors, but mostly of the man who was Vince Thornborough; the sensual odor was intoxicating. His beard was pleasantly rough under her fingers. "You need a shave," she whispered.

He made a move to pull back. "No, I like it." She stroked his chin again. "It's . . . titillating."

"Titillating, huh?" He growled and nipped at her earlobe.

Her hands moved over his back, his shoulders, his legs and arms, his belly, learning every plane and angle of his body by touch. Learning the smooth places, the hair-roughened spots and the work-roughened ones. Learning that if she touched here, a muscle would jump in response and he would inhale and grow tense or if she stroked him there he would relax with a sigh of pleasure.

He, in turn, was learning the same things about her—when she shivered with delight, when she moaned in ecstasy. He played with her, using his hands and his mouth, never quite hard enough, never in exactly the right place to let her reach a climax, but just enough to drive her wild.

She arched her back when he took her nipple into his mouth. She sighed when she felt his tongue, and whimpered as she felt the sharp, gentle edge of his teeth. She wiggled suddenly, and he loosened his grasp. Before he knew what was happening, she had urged him onto his back and was sprawled on top of him. She teased him then, lightly, smoothly, tauntingly, her clever fingers everywhere at once, until he was not only wild, he was begging. "Amanda!"

His hand slid between their bodies to touch her in the wet, warm center of her desire. She caught her breath at the exciting erotic sensation. Her voice was a hot whispered demand. "Now, Vince, please." He moaned and reversed their positions again.

He rose above her. His approach was slow and smooth and infinitely welcome. He knew he was heavy; he tried to hold his weight in check, but she didn't cooperate. Her nails dug into his shoulders, dragging him closer until he was buried deep within her.

He lost control. He found himself hammering into her. They swiftly, simultaneously, exploded into mercuric, impulsive motion. The rush, the flow, the excitement, the explosion together of two bodies in perfect balance and accord. Vince caught her head between his hands and covered her mouth hungrily.

He murmured her name, over and over. Finally, the drift, the flow of an ebbing tide, brought them naturally, effortlessly back to the present. Stillness, serenity, tranquillity, surrounded them.

Keeping Amanda securely in the curve of his arm, Vince reached for a blanket and covered them. The sexual tension, once so concentrated in the air between them, had snapped under the force of their lovemaking, leaving them relaxed and languid. They slept.

Like exhausted children, they slept.

Hours later, like exhausted children they awoke, touchy, testy, short-fused with each other.

Finally Vince caught her by the shoulders. He wanted to say something about the beauty of what they'd shared, but he was troubled about the experience, as well. He had no desire to get into anything complicated. His life was in enough of a mess without involvement.

And A.J. was frantic. Her feelings were too fiery, too intense. As long as she kept her distance, she'd been all right. But now distance had been eliminated. They had joined and become one person for a time.

There could be no future with this man, and she had never been one for casual sex. She thought people who slept together without any kind of commitment were foolish. She waited for Vince to say what he wanted to say, and then she was out of here. She'd go to the store or the library or to see May—anywhere to get out of this house for the rest of the day.

She could feel herself trembling. She tried to control it but she only made it worse.

"You're shaking. Amanda, did I hurt you?"

"No, of course not. I'm just—scared, I guess." When he frowned, she went on in a rush, "Not of you, Vince. Of myself."

He sighed and brought her into his arms. He rested his cheek on the top of her head and ran his big, warm hand soothingly down her back beneath her hair. "Yeah, I guess I am, too."

"That was pretty powerful stuff."

She could feel him smile, hear the smile in his voice. "It sure was."

"I'm not looking for anything that powerful, at least not—"

She broke off and he finished for her in a low, flat tone. "At least not from a military man."

"I was going to say, 'at least not right now.'"

"Were you?"

She didn't answer because she wasn't certain herself.

A.J. was in the kitchen when she thought she heard a car outside. She put down the spoon she was using to stir chili and headed for the back door.

But before she could get there Ed Wilson had walked in. Her face must have registered her surprise.

"I'm sorry, A.J. I should have called ahead," he said with charming politeness. "I'm so accustomed to dropping in without notice to take pot luck with Vince..." He spread his hands and lifted his shoulders in a gesture of helplessness.

She recovered quickly. "Certainly. Come in, Ed. If you like chili, you're in luck." She wished she were wearing something more formal than faded jeans and an oversize sweatshirt.

"Chili is one of my favorite dishes, especially when it's cold outside. The weather's changed on us." He followed her back to the main room, rubbing his hands together.

"Yes, it is getting colder."

When Sawdust came down the stairs to investigate, Ed scratched behind one ear. The dog permitted the touch for a moment but then he left to curl up in a corner, far from the humans.

"Vince, Ed's here," she called up the stairs. She wasn't sure what to do. Being around Ed Wilson still made her uncomfortable. Would the two men rather she disappear again?

She decided that she wasn't going to leave. "Have a seat, Ed." She sniffed, then wrinkled her nose when he walked past her. He smelled strange. Like he'd pumped his own gas and spilled it on his clothes. "If you'd like a drink or something, Vince can get it for you."

He went to the bar. "I can wait on myself," he said evenly.

"Oh, of course you can. Sorry. If you'll excuse me, I have to watch the chili," she said, returning to the kitchen.

A few minutes later, she was still putting the finishing touches on their meal when the telephone rang. "I'll get it in here," she called to the men who sat in front of the fireplace talking in low tones.

"Did you have your radio on? There was another fire this afternoon," said May without preamble. "I'm worried. This one was set in broad daylight and was much closer to us—over on Taylor Mountain."

"Thanks for calling, May. I'll turn it on right now." A.J. had turned the radio to an Atlanta station when she came into the kitchen an hour ago. She now switched the dial immediately to a local station. The fires seemed to be an ongoing story. This blaze had been discovered by a school bus driver on his way home from delivering his charges—at around four-thirty—and had destroyed about thirty acres on the south side of the mountain.

She called the two men to the table and told them about May's call. "I don't understand why they can't catch the man," she said impatiently as Vince held her chair.

"Maybe it's a woman," suggested Ed.

"The sheriff thought at first it was kids," Vince put in. "But now he's called in the Forest Service rangers. The person, of whatever gender, is lucky not to have been caught this time."

Ed nodded. "The sheriff's probably right. It sounds like kids. No one's been hurt, have they?"

"Not so far," Vince said. "But with every fire the law of averages increases the chances."

Every fire...every fire. Why did that phrase tickle her mind? Was there a pattern developing? She was frightened to think that someone could be hurt from the fires, but Vince's observation made sense to her.

When they were all seated, she shook out her napkin and placed it across her lap. "You'd better hope the sheriff doesn't drop by tonight, Ed. He'd probably be suspicious if he smelled the gasoline that was on your clothes when you came in."

"Amanda!" barked Vince. "That's a hell of a thing to say."

Ed had become very still. His expression was stark. "I filled my gas tank in town. The station closes early and I was afraid I'd need—"

"No one is accusing you," Vince cut him off.

"Of course not," A.J. agreed, silently cursing her own wayward tongue. "Please forgive me, Ed," she begged sincerely. "I hate self-serve. I always spill the gas on my clothes, too."

"Sure," Ed said with a laugh. "No offense taken."

But his laughter was nervous and unsteady. She felt responsible. He was Vince's friend, and she would put aside her silly prejudices and learn to like him. Just because he lacked finesse, he wasn't necessarily a villain.

"Shall we eat?" she said lightly in an attempt to defuse Vince's resentment. She had set the plates in the kitchen. Now she brought large bowls of her spicy chili and tossed salad to the table. She passed hot French loaves, sliced and seasoned with garlic butter. When she touched his arm, Vince took the basket and selected a piece of bread. But he didn't speak to her, didn't smile.

During the course of the meal, Ed put himself out to be charming and A.J. responded, finding that it wasn't as difficult as she'd thought it would be.

They had nearly finished when she noticed something that piqued her curiosity. Ed was constantly looking from one of them to the other, a puzzled frown on his handsome face. Could he tell by looking at them that a few hours ago they had been making passionate love upstairs? She knew instinctively that Vince would not want his buddies speculating about his relationship with her.

"Don't you think Vince looks better, Ed? He's been working out and he's gained some weight. Did he tell you about his training program?"

"No, he didn't tell me."

He was supposed to be such a good friend of Vince's; he should have noticed, thought A.J. She could tell that his pleased reaction at Vince's progress was forced.

"That's great, really great, buddy. How is your vision? Can you see anything yet?"

A.J. shot him a look.

"No, not yet," Vince answered without expression.

It was odd but even in casual conversation, Ed seemed to point out all the things Vince could not do, rather than encouraging the things he could. He did it with the utmost subtlety. Praise out of one side of his mouth, emphasize an imperfection out of the other side. She smiled to herself, wondering how Ed would react if she told him that in bed Vince was the A-number-one champ.

She saw Ed's frown deepen and returned her attention to the conversation. Vince was suggesting that, while her visit lasted, it wouldn't be necessary for him to make so many trips from Marietta. "You're welcome anytime, Ed, but I know it eats into your social life," he said.

"It's only a two-hour drive, old buddy," responded Ed. "You know me, I like to get away from the base every chance I get."

"And you know how much I appreciate your coming up here. You've been a real friend."

Ed laughed self-consciously. "You'd do the same for me."

"Believe it. Now tell me, what's the scuttlebutt in the squadron?"

A.J. tuned them out again as they began discussing people she had never met. Her thoughts returned to Ed and his attitude toward Vince's progress. Why wouldn't Ed be happy that his friend was adjusting and growing stronger? Or was she imagining his position? Was she allowing her long-seeded prejudice against the man to color her objectivity?

A.J. left the men alone after dinner, first dawdling in the kitchen, then going upstairs to her bedroom to read. Vince's relief when she said good-night was easy to interpret. He was still aggravated over her comment about the gas, and she wasn't sure she blamed him. She shouldn't have been so quick to say what she was thinking.

At ten o'clock, she was in bed with the lights off when she heard Ed's car engine start. A few minutes later Vince came upstairs. His footsteps hesitated then continued down the hall toward her room.

She held her breath waiting for a knock that would have been barely audible over her drumming heart. She wanted to fly to the door, to throw it open and welcome him into her arms.

Instead, she bit her lips together and remained quiet. He'd been genuinely angry and her wisest course would be to let him cool down a bit. But if he came to her...

She held her breath, waiting. After a minute, she heard his footsteps return him to his own room. She squeezed her eyes shut.

The following morning, Vince was up and dressed before A.J. He had prepared breakfast—oatmeal with cinnamon, escalloped apples that she had peeled and seasoned yesterday and buttered toast.

She walked into the sweet cloud of delectable smells. "This looks delicious." She took her stool beside his and started in on the breakfast.

"Thanks."

A.J. knew exactly what he was doing. He was demonstrating once again that he could take care of himself. That he didn't need her. That hurt for some reason, more deeply than it should have. She didn't want him to be dependent on her, did she? What a horrifying concept to emerge from the mind of a doctor.

"I'm going into town today to pick up a few things," A.J. said when they'd finished eating. "Would you like to go along?"

"No, thanks. More coffee?"

A man of few words. "Please." He refilled their cups.

She propped her elbows on the counter and sipped the hot coffee. "Vince, I'm really sorry if I insulted Ed last night."

He turned on her, his anger rekindled. "Amanda, how could you say such a thing? You practically accused him of setting the damned fires."

"I didn't," she protested.

"That's what it sounded like to me. Ed's visits have kept me sane."

She dropped her eyes to the coffee mug cradled between her hands. "I know. I'm really sorry."

Vince ate silently for a few minutes. At last he said, "Ed Wilson has no motive to set fires in these mountains." He paused. "Do you think he's a pyromaniac?"

"Of course I don't." She set down her cup with a thump. "Vince, please, can we drop the subject? I've apologized."

"It's a coincidence, that's all."

She swung her head in his direction. "What is?"

"That he's been here each time the fires were set."

When she didn't answer immediately, he repeated, "He has no motive."

Vince let himself be persuaded to take a walk around the lake with the dog. "Okay, okay, Dusty. Let me get the leash."

Dusty gave a loud woof and led the way across the back porch.

Vince was feeling guilty. He knew he had acted like a sullen bastard this morning. But, hell, she'd insulted his best friend. She'd provoked a suspicion even in him. He'd inadvertently searched his memory, put together the times of Ed's visits and been left with a bad taste of disloyalty in his mouth.

She might as well get the message right now. Even though they had made wonderful, glorious love to each other, he didn't belong to her any more than she belonged to him. He wasn't going to allow her to cut him off from his life or his friends.

She wasn't going to dictate his life. Sure, she'd gotten him started on a good exercise routine. He was stronger, had more stamina, more confidence in his own body. And he was grateful to her for prodding him. He prized the rapid improvement he was making; he felt like a different man already.

If he had to exercise, he would exercise, but he'd do it on his terms.

As he judged it, they had traveled about halfway around the lake when disaster suddenly struck. He had no warning.

Dusty set up a playful barking. Vince started to say something. Then he felt a hard jerk, and the leash was gone. Instinct and momentum carried him a number of steps in the same direction. Off the path. He whirled . . . lost his orientation.

He let out a stream of curses that would have blistered the ear of any rap star. Then he froze, turning only his head to follow the sound of barking. He would never know what had happened—had a rabbit or a fox appeared?—but the dog was off in full pursuit.

A helpless feeling washed over him. His worst nightmare came to life.

Not that he was in any danger, he reminded himself. Amanda had only gone to town. Eventually she would return to the cabin, find him missing and begin to look.

But right now he'd rather be unarmed and face an enemy plane than have her discover him helplessly wandering in the woods. He wanted her to see him with at least a semblance of assurance, confidence. In her eyes he wanted to appear powerful and rugged, masculine. Not timid or weak.

His frustration threatened his good sense, and he forced himself to breathe evenly, deeply, and consider the situation. Should he stand here waiting for the stupid dog to come back for him? Or should he take a chance on finding his way?

Hell, he could do it. All he had to do was find the path again. His sense of touch could keep him there. As long as he could feel hard-packed surface beneath his feet he should be fine. Nothing could happen.

If he found the path.

Chapter 8

It took Vince ten minutes to find the damned path. What followed was a harrowing hour.

Dusty finally decided to rejoin him just as the sound of Amanda's car reached his ears. Vince breathed a grateful sigh and grabbed for the leash as the dog started barking again. "Be quiet, Dusty," he ordered firmly. "She doesn't have to know everything."

He tried to present a casual appearance as he let the dog lead him the rest of the way to the cabin. When he entered, he could hear her in the kitchen, opening and closing the refrigerator, putting away cans in the pantry. He joined her there.

"Hi," she said in a low, hesitant tone.

Her voice sent an instant erotic chill up his spine, and the sultry memory of the touch of her skin clouded his brain. "Hi."

"Look at the two of you. You must have had a really heavy workout."

He nodded, making himself smile in her general direction. "We went for a long walk," he said to explain his sweaty shirt. He frowned. "What do I smell?"

"I just bought chrysanthemums, but they don't have a perfume."

It's you. It's your perfume, your naturally fresh and sensual scent. "No, but they smell nice. Fresh and natural."

"I couldn't resist. They're nice healthy plants, four pots of yellow blooms and four pots of the reddish bronze color. I'm going to plant them near the lake path."

"John won't exactly be crazy about that," he drawled as he bent down to unhook the leash.

"You're probably right. But maybe once he sees them in the ground, he'll like them."

Vince's fingers brushed something scratchy; he realized that the dog's coat was covered in briars. "Boy, you're a mess. If you'll hand me the brush, Amanda, I'll take him out to the mudroom and clean him up."

"You two must have gotten off the path."

Vince made a noncommittal noise. She gave him the brush, and he left her putting groceries away.

A.J. folded the paper bags and stored them in a bin in the pantry. She was thoughtful, her movements automatic. Something had obviously happened. Just as obviously, Vince wasn't going to tell her what it was. She shrugged—if that was the way he wanted it, that was how it would be. Whatever had happened, he was all right. When she was through with her small chores, she followed him to the mudroom off the carport.

Vince heard Amanda's footsteps. They slowed. He continued brushing the dog.

She paused on the threshold. "You're not mad at me any longer?"

Vince almost laughed out loud. He'd completely forgotten he was supposed to be angry. Over the past months, anger had become a too-familiar emotion in his life. Anger against fate had kept him going in the face of his blindness, his loss of memory, The Headache and the other, more minor, injuries. Now the anger seemed to have faded from his mind without his having noticed.

He shook his head and tried to maintain a mild expression. "No, I'm not mad. I may have overreacted. Besides, you apologized to Ed."

She hesitated. "Good," she said. "What do you want for dinner?"

Several days later, Vince lay on his bed, dressed only in his jeans, ankles crossed and hands stacked beneath his head, thinking about Amanda. His thoughts were complex, like she was.

The past few weeks had changed his opinion about her—he no longer pictured her as he remembered, a pretty, if spoiled, adolescent. He was most definitely impressed by the kind of woman she had become, and the impression had changed the mental image he had of her.

He was also sexually intrigued, no doubt about that. Though there had been no repeat of their lovemaking, his memory was active, often too active. She was fascinating, exciting, seductive. Their bodies together—it had been an extraordinary experience.

He took in a long breath and let it out. The aftermath had been predictable and probably for the best. They were both safer this way. Neither of them saw any future in continuing a relationship. They could easily get in too deep and as for any committed emotion, his sentiments were certain and sure. He and Amanda might as well have been standing at opposite poles when he considered the things they wanted out of life.

He couldn't afford deeper involvement, not until a conclusion was reached concerning his future. Hell, not even then. Since he had been old enough to understand the concept of flying, he'd known that was what he had to do with his life. Her profession demanded an equal commitment.

Right now, he was in limbo. But he had to be grateful for what she had done for him. He had been too satisfied to hibernate here, alone, waiting for his own personal miracle to take him back to where he belonged.

However, there was another side to this relationship coin, one they'd never found it necessary to discuss. Each of them clearly enjoyed the company of the other.

Her descriptions of things he could not see were vivid and insightful. They both enjoyed all kinds of music, from classical to country, but they were both addicted to rhythm and blues. They liked the same books. Neither of them watched much television.

And though they were trying to keep their relationship on a friendly level, a subtle but unmistakable tension remained in the air, a tension that only ebbed when he was physically exhausted.

Miracles rarely happened without a lot of sweat. John was right to take Amanda's side about the exercise program, and she was working him hard.

He moved his head restlessly. He wasn't being fair to her. He was working *himself* hard. Once he'd become dedicated to the program, he faced the routine with his own rigid inflexibility. Under her schedule, as opposed to the hit-or-miss regimen he'd followed before, he could measure the success himself.

The Headache had only bothered him twice in the past week, and a couple of aspirin had dispensed with the pain. He was up to forty push-ups a day.

With Dusty's help he jogged around the lake. As long as he had the dog to direct him back toward the cabin—and kept a firm grip on the leash—he was all right. He pictured himself jogging round and round, never knowing where to stop, where to get off.

The telephone rang beside his bed, interrupting his reverie. "Hello."

"Hi."

He smiled as he sat up, one foot on the floor, the other knee bent. "Hi. I was just thinking about you."

"You were?"

"Yeah. The dumb dog dug up your chrysanthemums."

She moaned. "Why didn't you stop him?"

"How the hell was I supposed to know what he was doing? He brought me one in his teeth."

"Okay." She sighed.

"How are things going?"

"I haven't been too encouraged so far. I wonder if I'll ever find the right place. One thing I know—the hospital I saw today wasn't it."

Vince wondered if she really knew what she was looking for. He also wondered if she'd followed up on May's suggestion that she talk to the local hospital.

"How many push-ups did you do today?" she asked.

Vince had been hoping she would ask; he grinned. "Forty. And this morning Dusty and I jogged around the lake."

"You're kidding me. Jogged, not walked?" She sounded pleased.

"A slow jog." He lay back against the pillows and smiled. "We're going to have to figure something out so I'll know when the path passes the cabin."

She was quiet for a minute. "Take the radio out on the porch and turn it on loud."

He laughed softly. "Why didn't I think of that?"

"What about the weight machine?"

"You're a hard taskmaster, Doc. I pressed eighty pounds."

"Vince, that's wonderful," she said, her husky voice velvety to his ears. "I wish I'd been there to see it."

His voice dropped an octave. "I wish you had been here, too. What time will you be back?"

"I'm not sure. The administrator I met with today insisted on turning me over to the medical auxiliary. They took me to lunch, then showed me the neighborhoods, the shopping, the schools. They invited me for dinner, but I begged off. I didn't get to the motel until a few minutes ago."

He touched his watch. It was after seven. "But you didn't like the place?"

"Dalton is a lovely little city with a substantial manufacturing base for their economy. But they don't need me, Vince. They have plenty of doctors, a hospital with up-to-the-minute equipment. No, I'm looking for something smaller, where I can make a difference. On my way home tomorrow I'm going to stop off in Blue Ridge."

Her statement gave him more food for thought. Though City Hospital was in a large urban area, their problems were even larger. They had needed her. Then she'd come to the cabin where she'd started right in on him. Trying to make a difference. He'd given her hell, but she'd kept at it. "I think I understand," he said. To be needed was very important to her.

"Do you? I wish I did," she said. He could hear the weariness in her voice.

"Get yourself something to eat and go to bed," he ordered gruffly. "Start taking care of *yourself* for a change. And that's an order."

"Yes, Major." The weariness was replaced by laughter. "See you tomorrow."

When Vince hung up, he kept his hand on the receiver for a minute, as though reluctant to break off contact. At least he'd made her feel better.

The dream returned that night. Vince awoke drenched in sweat, with the sound of his own shout echoing in his ears.

The dog nuzzled his hand, whining softly. "Thanks, Dusty. I'm okay."

But he wondered. There was more to the dream this time, and he strained to remember. Tanks. With the inverted V of the allies painted clearly on their sides. Had he shot at friendly tanks? He shook his head to clear it, then caught the sides in his palms. No, God, no. Surely he hadn't fired on allied tanks. But no one could be found who had seen him in the hectic five minutes prior to the crash.

The next morning he called John and asked him to come for the weekend. "Bring the crash reports, will you?"

"Have you remembered something?" John asked.

"Not enough," answered Vince.

The next evening A.J. drove steadily, eager to get back to the cabin. Two days away from Vince and Dusty were two days too long. She avoided examining the reasons for such thinking.

It was twilight when she came to the turnoff. She was stunned to be halted by a roadblock. "What...?" She rolled down the window as the sheriff approached her car. "Sheriff?"

"Hello, Dr. Upton. If you'll wait just a minute, we'll let you through."

"What happened? Is everything all right at the cabin? Vince—?"

"The grove of trees on the lake at your dad's cabin was burned."

Her throat closed painfully. "That close?" she whispered.

"I'm afraid so. We thought we had the arsonist this time. A helicopter spotted the fire before it had a chance to spread. We put up roadblocks on all the access roads immediately. But unless he's still in there, we lost him again.''

"And you haven't had any luck?"

"'Fraid not.''

"Do you still think it's kids?''

"No, I don't. If this started out as a lark, it's turnin' into a more serious problem. Eventually someone's gonna get hurt if we don't stop this." He took off his hat and used his sleeve to wipe perspiration from his brow, though the evening breeze was chilly. He looked over to his men, who had moved the barrier. "You can go through now." He stepped back from the car and waved her on.

He looked so discouraged. She felt sorry for him. Nevertheless she broke all speed limits getting back to the cabin. She had the car door open before she thrust the gear shift into Park. "Vince! Vince!" she shouted. The house was empty.

Her apprehension grew as she went from room to room calling his name. At last she went back outside, noticing for the first time the faint smell of smoke in the air. "Vince!" she yelled again.

"Around here," she heard him call and felt a wave of relief.

She turned at the corner of the house and saw him, kneeling in the dirt. Her breath was suddenly threatened by the large, dry lump in her throat. He had replanted her chrysanthemums and a hose leaked water onto their bedraggled stems. Nearby, Dusty barked joyfully, but he was secured by the leash and the leash had been wedged between the drainpipe and the house.

Vince rose, wiping his muddy hands on his faded jeans. His old torn sweatshirt was covered in dirt. He'd never looked so good to her. With no hesitation, she walked into his arms. "Where were you when the fire started? God, I've never been so scared in my life. The sheriff said the fire was on the other side of the lake. You could have been jogging there. Where—" He cut her off by the simple expediency of covering her mouth with his. But there was something ... detached about his kiss. The arms that held her seemed rigid, inflexible.

"God, I missed you," he said, softening at last. He pulled off her knitted cap, releasing her hair. He buried his hand in the glorious mass and kissed her again. This time the kiss was hungry, almost desperate.

A.J. pressed against him, her arms clamped around his waist. He felt so strong, so substantial. Her relief was almost overwhelming.

Neither of them noticed that the dog was jumping around them, trying for his own share of attention, until he barked, sharply, and continued to bark until A.J. broke away and released his leash.

Vince was reluctant to let her go. She dropped to her knees to give the dog a proper greeting. "Dusty, you're a good boy. Did you miss me?"

"Where's your suitcase?" asked Vince.

"In the back seat," she answered, getting to her feet again. "Down, Dusty."

Vince took her bag from the car. He hooked his hand to her elbow and they went into the cabin.

"The sheriff said the fire burned the trees on the other side of the lake," A.J. said as they entered the main room. She peeled off her jacket and dropped it along with her purse on a nearby chair as she crossed to the window. The lovely little grove was a black smear against the mountain. "Oh, God, Vince," she breathed, turning away from the sight. Her heart was pounding. "He says he doesn't think it's kids. He says this is something much more serious than a lark."

"I know. He told me," Vince answered. "Let's don't talk about the fire, okay?"

She remembered looking at the glorious colors and thinking how pretty the dogwoods would be in the spring. The lake had been still; the trees had been reflected on its surface. Now the only reflection was of twisted, leafless, blackened trunks.

She turned back to Vince, suddenly aware of the withdrawal in his voice. "But it was so close," she said, aware of her own weak-kneed feelings at the thought of the danger.

"Yeah, the smoke drifted this way for a while, but the wind changed. Ed was here when it happened."

"Ed was here?" she asked softly.

"May came over, and the sheriff, too." He didn't comment on her question. "I was well looked after," he said, his expression hard.

"Don't." She returned to his side. "Please don't resent them, Vince. They wanted to help."

"Ah, hell. I appreciate their concern. It's just that I'm so damn restless." He whirled on her. "I don't want you to think I don't appreciate all you've done, Amanda...." He began to pace.

"If I could make you understand ... It was hard as hell to do, but I had learned to handle things on my own. Now I can feel myself growing dependent again and I don't like it. I was patient before. Now I'm impatient." He raked his fingers through his already disheveled hair. "Before, I didn't have to count on anyone except May. And I was paying her."

"Then I arrived," A.J. continued for him in an even voice, but she was annoyed. She thought they had progressed beyond this kind of resentment. "'Get out in the fresh air, Vince. Eat more and exercise, Vince.' Am I characterizing it right?"

His head came up with a jerk. His eyes narrowed behind the tinted glasses. "Yeah," he said guardedly. "I guess I'm just edgy."

"You haven't gotten the point yet, have you?" she said, unable to hide her irritation any longer. "Well, I'm sorry you don't like it, Major." She swiped at her jacket and purse. "You weren't really independent, you were just dependent on fewer people. But you rarely went to town or even outside of the cabin.

"I wasn't content to let you hibernate. And neither was my father. The message here is that the people who *really* care about you *wanted* you to be impatient." She strode to the steps and picked up her suitcase. "I'm going to have a shower."

"I apologize for blowing up earlier," said A.J., laying her hand on his leg. They had finished dinner and were sitting side by side in front of the fireplace, their shoulders not quite touching. Della Reese's mellow voice and syncopated music made its way softly through the room. "It's just that I was so glad to see you safe, and then you reacted like our attempts to keep you that way were all part of a stupid conspiracy."

Vince covered her hand with his and raised it to his lips. He kissed her palm, touched it with his tongue.

"I'm sorry, too. And I am grateful, no matter what I say."

"I don't want your gratitude." Her husky voice was low and sexy. She rubbed her fingers across his jaw where the skin was beard-rough. "You haven't shaved today."

The rasp set up an erotic tremor, beginning in his stomach and radiating outward. He bent his head to find a tender spot on her throat and returned their clasped hands to his leg. He moved them in slow strokes along his thigh. "And you've let your hair down. Are we trying to tell each other something?"

"Yes," she spoke softly. "I'm trying to say I'm glad to be back here with you. Are you glad?"

"God, yes. I told myself a hundred times that we had been wise, that we'd made a sound, sensible decision to stop any physical intimacy before the feelings became too intense, too powerful."

She rested her head on his shoulder. "I don't feel like being sensible any longer, Vince. I think we should face this relationship in an entirely different way. We should enjoy being together. I'm very attracted to you."

"And you, Doctor, are too sexy to ignore. You smell too good, your skin is too soft and the sound of your voice is like an erotic massage down my spine. Last night, on the phone—hell, by the time you hung up, I wanted you." He dropped her hand and pulled her beneath the curve of his arm.

She felt the adrenaline shoot through her veins, laughed at the exciting sensation and freed her arms from between their bodies to wind them around his

neck. She deliberately fell backward on the soft cushions of the sofa, bringing him down on top of her.

"Wait, babe..."

He tried to put the brake on their movements, to
take it slow and easy, but she shifted her hips under
him and sent him into orbit. His hands sought the
buttons of her blouse. Impatiently he freed them, then
covered her breasts with his big hands. He lowered his
mouth to her, murmuring her name against her soft
skin.

Moments later their clothes were gone, strewn all
over the floor, the table. She was slick and ready for
him. She laughed again as he slid inside her.

He caught his breath. "That feels...ah..." He ex-
haled. "Interesting."

"What does?" she whispered, moving beneath him
impetuously.

His hands grasped her hips. "When you laugh—it
feels—oh, Amanda..." And then he couldn't speak
anymore.

Hours later they lay together in Vince's big bed.

"What brought Ed back?" asked A.J., her husky
voice subdued.

"He wanted to tell me that he's gotten orders for
California."

"When does he leave?"

"In a couple of weeks." He turned toward her and
cupped her cheek in his big hand. "Tell me about the
town you saw today. Was it a place you liked?"

He was trying to shift the subject and she let him,
for the moment, anyway. "Blue Ridge. It's in the
mountains about forty miles from here. I was there for

hours and there was no activity in the emergency room at all, not a single case. I'm not sure their hospital needs a full-time ER specialist. However, it's a beautiful little town and a definite possibility.''

''No corporate owners?''

''No.'' She laid her hand on his warm chest. His heartbeat was strong and steady. ''Vince, we can't ignore this coincidence with Ed Wilson any longer. We've got to tell the sheriff.'' She hated to raise the subject, but her conscience wouldn't let her ignore it, either.

Vince dropped his hand and lay flat on the bed beside her. She turned on her side and propped her head on her hand to look at him. His expression was somber but there was no anger, no outrage, as there had been when the subject was mentioned before.

He was silent for a long time. Finally he sighed heavily. ''Don't take this wrong, Amanda,'' he began.

She interrupted with a chuckle. ''I've always found that people who begin a sentence with that phrase are about to tell you something you don't want to hear.'' She studied his profile while she waited.

''Yeah, well, you're right, you're not going to want to hear this. Especially since I said we'd put the past behind us,'' he said with a wry twist of his lips. ''Amanda, I learned fourteen years ago how devastating it can be to have your reputation rest on a false accusation. Ed was here—there was another fire. Even I am beginning to wonder.'' He stopped, took a breath and let it out. ''But for the life of me, I can't come up with a motive. And until I can, I won't make such an

accusation to anyone in authority. I don't think you
would want to, either.''

With his first sentence she felt the blood drain from
her face. She raised herself and sat cross-legged, staring down at him. By the time he'd finished she was
light-headed and her cheeks were flooded with heat.
She put one hand over her eyes. This was not the argument she'd anticipated. "No, I wouldn't want that
to happen again," she said hoarsely.

"But you're offended."

Her hand dropped loosely to the mattress. "No,
that isn't it at all. I understand your feelings. I should
have seen the connection myself."

She wondered what Vince would say if she told him
the whole truth about Ed. If Ed had been man enough
fourteen years ago, he could have cleared Vince of all
suspicion immediately. She opened her mouth, but
before she could say anything, he spoke.

"I'll admit my suspicions are aroused. And I swear
to you, Amanda, I'll be the first person to tell the
sheriff when the time is right. But I have to have more
information. I've racked my brain but for the life of
me I cannot come up with a rational reason for Ed's
having started the fires."

She closed her mouth again, satisfied with his
promise. "All right." She shook her head sadly, swung
her feet to the floor and stood up. "This conversation
makes me wonder if I've learned anything in the past
fourteen years."

"Stop it," he snapped and held out his hand.
"Come back here."

She touched his fingers briefly. "I need to think, Vince. And I can't do that when I'm in your bed. I'll see you in the morning." She left.

The next morning, A.J. faced the fact that she had welcomed Vince into her arms, and now she was beginning to wonder if she could keep him out of her heart. Her emotions were mercurial, slipping and sliding from a glorious high to the depths of dismay. It was all very well to suggest they should enjoy each other while they were together, but what would happen when they parted?

She wasn't quite ready to admit to herself that she was falling in love with him. But after last night, she knew she was close. She would have disappeared immediately after breakfast if Vince had allowed it.

But he was adamant in his determination not to let her draw away from him. He touched her whenever she was within arm's reach. He kissed her often, he teased her and made her laugh. And they talked. They talked about everything except Ed Wilson.

It was a rare Indian summer day. The sky was an unbelievable blue. The radio had warned, however, that a storm front was moving in, one which could bring the first snowfall of the season.

Vince suggested they take their lunch outside and spread a blanket on the beach to take advantage of the good weather. They ate turkey sandwiches and potato chips and drank hot coffee from a thermos.

At last, Vince lay back replete, his hands under his head, his legs crossed at the ankle. A feeling of contentment fell over him. He was alert as he lay under the bright sky.

He'd begun to feel that the black world he'd lived in for so long seemed less intense. There was no actual sense of light, just a slight lifting of the darkness. He was afraid to hope, afraid to wish for an end to this nightmare.

But he couldn't hide his excitement completely.

"Are you asleep?" Amanda asked.

"No. Just daydreaming."

"When did you plan to tell me?"

He turned his head in her direction. The wind ruffled his hair. "You know?"

"I know that something has excited you, that you don't hear what I'm saying because you're distracted. And a couple of times this morning, you've forgotten to put on your glasses."

He put out his hand, palm up. She placed hers in it and he held on tightly. He was disinclined to speak the thought out loud. "I wasn't sure. The darkness is— how can I describe it? It's less intense. That's all."

She closed her eyes for a minute. "Oh, Vince," she breathed. "That's wonderful." She started to pick up the remains of their meal, stuffing them into the picnic basket. "Come on."

"Hey, calm down. What are you doing?"

She tugged at the hand he still held. "Let's go call your physician. Maybe he can see you before the end of the week."

He got to his feet and brought her up with him. But he didn't let go of her hand and when she would have headed immediately for the cabin and the telephone, he stopped her. "Not yet," he said.

"Why?"

"It isn't enough."

"Yes, it is enough. I'm a doctor. I know that any progress, no matter how light, should be reported immediately."

He dropped her hand but only to draw her into the circle of his arms. "Then, Doctor, let's put me under observation for a few days," he said, teasing her. His hands moved restlessly up her sides, over her back. "Let's see if the light gets any stronger."

She laid her cheek on his broad chest and wound her arms around his waist, hooking her thumbs in the band of his jeans. "I don't understand you, Vince. I thought you'd be wild with joy."

He sobered and squeezed her shoulder. "Aside from the fact that I don't want to get my hopes up and have them crushed, I'll have to go back into the hospital, Amanda." He shrugged. "I'm not ready to give you up yet."

She understood. The day he began to regain his sight would mark the end of their stay at the cabin. Selfishly, she would like for this idyll to last forever, but practically that was impossible.

"Besides, your father is coming up next weekend."

"You didn't tell me that."

"I called him to bring the crash reports. Maybe there will be something in them to stimulate my memory."

"Did you tell him about the light?"

"No, I don't want anyone to know until I'm convinced I'll see clearly again." His features hardened; a muscle quaked in his jaw. "Pity can be a tedious emotion, and I don't want to have to experience it all over again if this turns out to be a false hope."

She started to argue, but his expression stopped her. "I suppose we should alert May, invite her to dinner," she said instead.

"What do you want to bet John's already invited her?" he asked with a chuckle, then his expression grew solemn. "Let's wait until next Monday to call the doctor in Atlanta. Okay, Tiger?" He ruffled her hair, then his fingers closed, making a fist. He tugged gently to tilt her head back. His lips were warm on hers. "Okay?" he repeated huskily.

"You're using unfair coercion, Major."

"Please?"

"If I don't make an appointment, may I just call and talk to him?"

"What for?"

"Professional courtesy? And I can find out what to expect—what kind of time frame we're looking at, things like that." She wasn't sure he'd buy it, but he did.

"All right, you can call. But don't make an appointment, and don't tell anyone else."

"Okay," she breathed. Then he was kissing her again, hungrily.

Amanda and her father hadn't gotten along particularly well when he was here before, and she wasn't looking forward to his return. She admitted as much to Vince that night as they lay in each other's arms. "I wonder if he'll criticize your recuperation. You've clearly made great progress building up your strength, but if I know John, he'll find something wrong."

Vince ran his hand down her spine and back up again. "Hey, Tiger, it'll be two against one. I'm satisfied with my progress, and so are you. Besides, John won't be here for several days.''

"Several days longer for me to worry.''

"Don't you dare set up a quick interview and run out on me.''

She laughed and scooted closer. She hooked one leg over his thigh and moved her head from his shoulder to his broad chest. She loved to hear the reassuring beat of his heart under her cheek. "How did you know that was what I was thinking?'' she asked him softly.

"You are not a coward, Tiger,'' he stated instead of answering her question. "You're a beautiful, intelligent, accomplished woman. Your only hang-up is your relationship with your father. When you first arrived here you told me you were indifferent to John, yet after five minutes of conversation with him, you raised your defenses.''

"I did not,'' she protested, making a fist and hammering lightly on his chest. Then she added, "I didn't mean to.''

"He's used to giving orders. Don't let him intimidate you.''

She sighed. "I'll try.''

Vince was fully aware of the conflict going on within Amanda. She wasn't as emotionally indifferent to John as she had wanted him to think, but she was still hesitant to open up completely. She didn't want to put her heart on the line.

He couldn't blame her. John had been like a father to him, but he'd also been on the receiving end of the older man's anger fourteen years ago. The man was larger than life, a legend in the air force. He expected the best from his men and women, and for the most part, he got the best.

But Vince knew how it felt to let John Upton down.

His arm tightened briefly, protectively around Amanda's shoulders. She made a small sound, then sighed. He smiled as he realized that she'd fallen asleep. His fingers slid softly through her hair. He would like to see her reconciled with her father, and he had a feeling it might happen.

He cared for her—he'd known that for a while. While his emotions were not completely defined, they were steadily growing in intensity, making him want to shield her from any pain. He'd discovered over the past weeks that Amanda was more important to him than any of the casual relationships he'd had with other women.

On one or two occasions he'd started to open up, to tell her how he felt, but he'd held back.

Her animosity toward military life and her own genuinely vital career stood between them like very large, very high walls. There was also the matter of his own future. Before he shared his feelings too freely, he'd better do some thinking.

What would happen to him if he couldn't fly again? He hadn't been able to face that question until the darkness had begun to lift. But now he had to deal with a reality that was fast approaching Mach 3.

He had an aeronautical engineering degree, which counted for something if he wanted to design or build planes. But he couldn't conceive of himself sitting behind a desk. Hell, he couldn't picture himself anywhere except where he belonged, in the cockpit of a plane.

Well, son, you'd better start picturing it. Chances were better than even that his vision would never be the same.

There. He'd actually thought the unthinkable. He might never fly again. He took in a long, deep breath and let it out slowly. The idea sat like an elephant on his chest.

Chapter 9

That night Vince had the dream again, and, as before, there was additional detail to the horror. He heard his own yell and sat straight up in bed, forcing himself out of the black depths of the nightmare, sweat drenching his shaking body.

But this time he was not alone.

Amanda was awakened by his thrashing. Heart pumping, she let out a small but audible gasp of her own before she realized what was happening. She quickly switched on the bedside lamp.

Vince's elbows were on his knees; his back was hunched; his hands covered his face. She could see him shaking, and his body was slick with perspiration.

He resisted when she tried to draw him into the warm circle of her arms. But finally he relaxed, and she lay down again, holding him tightly, as he was holding her.

"It's all right, Vince," she whispered, running her hand over his back in pacifying circles. "You're home now...not out there...not alone in the desert...you're right here in bed with me."

She kept up her soft, soothing murmur until he quit shaking. She found that she was trembling slightly herself. In all her years as a doctor she'd never felt this deep empathy with a convalescent. His fear seemed to be her fear; his pain, her pain.

He let go of a deep breath and rolled onto his back. The sheet settled across his lean hips. He slept naked; she wore one of his T-shirts.

When he spoke his voice was a harsh rasp. "Every time I have the dream, I see more of the picture, like a crazy Polaroid, where one corner develops, then the top, then another," he said. His breathing had steadied. "It would be a hell of a lot easier if the whole picture developed at once."

Amanda brushed the damp hair back from his forehead. His eyes were open, and his gaze was fixed on the ceiling. She wondered if the light was discernible to him, but this was not the time to ask. She realized that in his mind, he was still out in the desert. "Do you want to tell me about it?"

He shifted away from her. She lay on her side watching. "Are you sure you want to hear this? I don't even know how much is real and how much is the dream."

"Tell me," she urged quietly.

After a minute he began to speak, his voice an expressionless monotone. "The squadron is flying a sortie over the desert at the end of a very long day. The sun hangs over the horizon like a giant orange ball. It's hot—dear God, it's hot as hell. There is nothing but sand for as far as the eye can see. We have a specific target, a weapons plant that intelligence has told us is disguised as a burned-out hangar. The enemy are wizards at making one thing look like another. In and out—quick—that's our mission."

He laid his forearm over his eyes. "Not unexpectedly the squadron came under some antiaircraft fire. But then I saw one of our planes veer off into another sector away from where we were supposed to be. I wondered if his navigational equipment had malfunctioned. Everything was confused but not that confused." He rolled his head from side to side on the pillow.

A.J. wondered thoughtfully if he realized that he'd changed tenses—from the present tense of an ongoing dream to the past tense of a memory.

She could feel the agitation begin to build within him. She put her hand on his bare chest. His skin was cold to the touch and slightly clammy. His heart was pounding like a battering ram against his rib cage. But the doctor within her confirmed automatically that the beat was strong and regular.

"I had to go after him. Off to starboard I suddenly saw a big section of the sand lift up, and enemy tanks...dozens of enemy tanks crawling out of the hole in the sand like huge black insects." He took her hand off his chest and laid it carefully on the bed, retreating from her touch, from any comfort she might offer.

He went on. "The antiaircraft fire was hot and heavy, but, thank God, their aim was lousy. The tank missiles would be the real danger. My attention focused on the plane ahead of me. It was one of my men—I *had* to get him out of there. He didn't respond to any radio calls, and he was flying erratically, as though the machine itself was having a seizure of some kind.

"Then I saw another convoy of tanks. But these wore the distinctive inverted V that had been used to mark all allied equipment during the Gulf War. They must have been on patrol. I was glad to see them— they would engage the enemy tanks, distract their attention from us."

The muscle in his jaw jumped erratically. He held himself motionless, but she could tell the extraordinary effort it cost. She bit at her bottom lip and remained silent.

When he continued, his voice was without color, without emotion, as though he needed to withdraw, to distance himself from the rest of the recital. She soon realized why.

"I started to pull alongside him for a visual, when— without any warning, without any reason at all—the rogue fired two of its rockets at the *allied* convoy. The damn pilot—in an aircraft from *my* squadron, *my* responsibility—fired directly into the center of the allied task force, igniting ammunition, instantly incinerating men and equipment. God!

"One tank exploded immediately. Another caught fire. I could see the men, their clothes in flames, scrambling to escape from that flaming tomb. I could almost hear their screams. I could feel the heat searing, scorching their skin.

"The entire area was a blazing inferno. And I was screaming, too. I was screaming, 'Friendlies! Friendlies! Cease your attack.' I kept screaming and screaming, and he wouldn't stop. I felt a violent tremor rip through my bird. I guess that's when I was hit, but at the time it seemed like another dimension of my own shock. That's all. After that, everything is black." He inhaled and released the breath in a shuddering sigh. "They were Americans, Amanda. Americans..."

His eyes were still hidden beneath his arm. His voice had trailed off to a whisper. He lay straight beneath the sheet, gripping the fabric in his powerful fist. She knew better than to try to comfort him at this moment. He was in a nightmare of his own, one she could not enter, could not intrude upon.

Then she saw the tears seeping from under his forearm. They made a glistening path into his dark hairline.

Oh, God, no. She closed her eyes. She couldn't bear to see him weep. Her own tears escaped and tracked down her cheeks. She struggled and finally gained a semblance of control over her emotions, just a thread, but she clung to it as though it were a lifeline. Vince didn't need a Weeping Winnie.

He made no sound for a long time. He just lay there, mourning silently, internally, for the dying warriors in the flaming tanks.

She felt so helpless! Damn it, she was a doctor. And a woman. She should be able to take his pain, should be able to hold it away from him for a while, so he could rest from the burdensome weight.

But even if that were possible, she knew he would not allow it. She could only wait with him for the nightmare to be over.

Finally he spoke. "The ultimate betrayal," he said contemptuously. "I wonder how those kids felt. In the short time they had, did they realize they were being attacked by their allies?"

She put her hand to her lips to hold back a sob and stumbled to the bathroom where she filled a glass with water. She returned to the bed, rounded to the other side, sat down at his side. "Vince, it was just a dream. Sit up. Here, drink this." She used the flat, no-nonsense voice she used with a difficult patient.

He removed his arm and shook his head. Revulsion had ground the lines deeper into this face, honed the planes to a sharp edge. "No, no more drugs," he said lethargically, as though he'd said it many, many times before.

A.J. smiled crookedly. Then she touched his shoulder. "Sit up and drink this, dummy. It's water. Plain old water."

He sat up, drained the glass and gave it back to her. "Thanks." She put it on the bedside table. Then he lifted the covers. "I'm cold, Tiger. Come warm me up," he said softly.

A.J. turned off the bedside lamp and climbed in beside him, pulling the sheet and a blanket over them. She wrapped her arms around as much as she could of him and held on. Their faces were inches apart on the pillow. "It was just a dream," she repeated. Then she tucked her head under his chin and closed her eyes. They lay like that for a while, but Vince's skin was still cold and he hadn't relaxed.

At last, he spoke into the darkness. "Amanda, what if it isn't a dream? What if *I* was the pilot who freaked out? What if I fired those rockets at other Americans?''

She realized suddenly that this fear was the deepest, most formidable of all. Here was his nightmare—not the blindness, not the injuries, but the fear that he'd shot at and killed his countrymen. "You didn't," she said fiercely.

"How do you know? I don't. I can go only so far and then I come smack up against a dense black curtain. I can't see around or through it and it's so thick it suffocates me."

What could she say? How could she reassure him?

She drew away, propped her chin on one hand and looked at him. With her other hand she stroked his chest. His musculature was firm and growing noticeably stronger. Her eyes had adjusted to the small bit of starlight that came in through the window, and she could make out his features. His cheeks were no longer gaunt. He had regained almost all of his lost weight. Physically, he was nearly the same man he used to be.

And he had the mental strength to face this, too. She didn't doubt that for a minute. There would be difficult times to get through first. As a doctor, she knew he must not lose his confidence; he'd come too far. "Because I know you, Vince," she said simply.

His mouth curved in a bitter half smile, but he brought her closer for a brief but thorough kiss.

She melted against him, hoping the conversation was over, hoping he would put it out of his mind. Until he could remember everything there was no cause for him to torture himself.

But he was not finished. "Are you going to testify at my court-martial? Say you know me, and that I didn't do it?"

"Don't be silly. There isn't going to be any court-martial."

"There ought to be. I understand all the arguments, that in battle tragic mistakes are made, that we do everything humanly possible to avoid them, that we perfect our weapons, our delivery, our intelligence and we screen our manpower carefully.

"But this case is very different. In this instance orders were either ignored, suppressed or disobeyed. A pilot went berserk, deliberately left his assigned zone, his prescribed target."

"I've heard of 'friendly fire.' Accidents occur in battle. To us here at home, they are horrible, even unthinkable. But that pilot was not you," she said doggedly. "I know that you didn't break off from your squadron, you didn't go berserk, you didn't attack an allied target."

He chuckled then. "Thanks, Tiger."

"For believing in you?" she scoffed. "I don't deserve a medal for that. You've always been dedicated and determined."

He took her hand in his and brought it to his lips. "Thanks for listening, then. It's good to talk to someone besides military doctors."

She settled back into his arms. Slowly the tension ebbed from his body, and she felt him relax against her. She was drowsy herself, almost asleep, when she had a thought. "Vince?"

He shifted one leg across hers, bringing her closer. "Hmm?"

"In your dream did you ever get a visual—do you know who the other pilot was?"

He yawned. "Sometimes, when we're flying so close, I can almost see his face," he said, the sleep clearing from his voice. "But it's never quite clear enough."

At that moment she wanted to say something else to him. To her own surprise, she found that she wanted to tell him she'd fallen in love with him.

She knew exactly when it had happened. And she was very sure of her feelings.

Her heart swelled at the realization. She wanted to tell him; she wanted it so badly that she closed her eyes and clamped her lips together to keep the knowledge inside her. "I love you, Vince," she would have said. "And I will do whatever I can to make your handicap easier to bear." Her vow was silent, but it was no less sincere for not being spoken aloud.

She couldn't tell him of her feelings. Not right now. Maybe never. Such an admission at this time would only add to the pressure he felt.

He had never asked for anything more than her in his bed. He didn't want commitment, didn't want vows or promises, didn't want permanence.

She hadn't thought she'd wanted promises, either. So how could she tell him that she had known from the moment she'd returned to find the house empty? When faced with the prospect of life without him, she'd known instantly that she wanted a life with him.

Even so, there remained many other obstacles to a lasting relationship, not the least of which was his military career. She would not be a statistic, like her parents, in a lonely marriage—two nice people who should never have gotten together.

For now she would have to be content here in the darkness, in his arms.

"What time is it?" Vince asked.

She looked at her watch, but she couldn't see the dial. "I don't know. Does it matter?"

Vince's watch was on the bedside table. He stretched out his hand. "It's only twelve-thirty," he said. "It seems later."

"Vince?" she said, suddenly lifting her head.

"Hmm?"

"Did they locate your plane?"

"Yes, finally."

"Did it have any ordnance on it?"

"So you picked up on that, did you? Except for what I released over the target, it was all accounted for. That's why I'm not in custody right now."

She felt excitement at the news. "Then why can't they go the other way? Find out which planes came back empty?"

He tightened his arms and laughed softly into the darkness. "Because, my dear, sweet advocate, the squadron ran into enemy aircraft on the way back to the base. A dogfight ensued and by the time it was over, *no* one had ordnance left. Let's get some sleep."

Vince awoke before Amanda. Careful not to disturb her, he reached out to touch his watch. Almost 7:00 a.m. He was surprised. He hadn't slept for that long a stretch since the crash.

He slid his free hand under his head, feeling rested, revived, at peace. It was a hell of a good feeling, and he owed it all to this slender bundle curled up against his side.

He kept forgetting how small Amanda was, how slender and delicate and dainty. But her heart wasn't small; it was huge. She could listen without being judgmental and respond with the right degree of warmth and thoughtfulness. Hell, she'd been there before he even realized he needed anything or anyone.

She'd held him and made him talk about the nightmare as more of it was revealed. Talking seemed to have acted as a catharsis on his pent-up emotions. This morning he felt lighter, as though he'd set down a heavy trunk he hadn't been aware of carrying.

She stirred in his arms. He placed his lips to the tender spot on her temple. He could feel her pulse beating there and the pastoral scent of her shampoo filled his nostrils. She snuggled closer, her sweet body warm against his.

Odd, he'd never thought a feeling of contentment was sexy. But he found it very sexy just to hold her next to him. Not that he didn't want her, he thought with a wistful smile. He'd have to be dead not to. But he was patient. He'd wait until she woke up. The smile became a grin. Maybe.

"What time is it?" she asked in a voice thick with sleep.

"Time to wake up," he murmured. He rolled toward her, his hand seeking the warmth between her thighs. He moved her hair off her neck and replaced it with his lips. "Time for a morning workout. It's seven o'clock."

She arched her back, warm and pliable and responsive in his arms. "What kind of workout did you have in mind?" she asked in that sexy, whiskey voice.

Before he could answer, she stiffened. "Yikes!" She sat up. "Did you say seven o'clock? I have an appointment at nine."

He hooked an arm around her waist and dragged her back into his embrace. "That's two hours from now. You have plenty of time," he said gruffly.

"The hospital's an hour away. I have to shower and dress," she protested. But the protest held no real conviction.

He'd found the hem of the T-shirt she was wearing and began to work it slowly, tortuously up her body. "Then let me help you," he said huskily. By the time the shirt hit the floor, her arms were wrapped around his neck and her tongue was mating with his in a sensually undulating dance of desire.

She was only ten minutes late.

"Vince, tell me, am I too hard to please?"

A.J. had returned from her appointment at lunchtime. She couldn't explain why she'd cut the interview short. She'd given the administrator a patently weak excuse, left the hospital and driven straight back to the cabin.

Vince had already eaten so she'd slapped a sandwich together for herself and poured a glass of milk. Now she took a big bite and chewed thoughtfully while she waited for him to answer.

He set aside the towel he'd been using on the counter and came to join her on the other side of the passthrough. "Amanda, you may not like what I'm about to say, but think about it carefully for a minute. You were suffering from burnout when you arrived here. For several years, without any break at all, you had been a part of a grisly, devastating side of life. You had witnessed things that no human being should have to bear—it was similar to warfare. Worse, you'd had to repair the wounds and ease the suffering. You were devastated and depressed. And you felt you needed a complete change of life-style. Am I right so far?''

She nodded, swallowed the bite of sandwich and said, ''Yes, you're right,'' wondering where this was leading.

''But you're resilient and you soon began to heal. You enjoyed the quiet here at the cabin, and there was no pressure on you. You rested. You exercised in the fresh mountain air—I'm willing to bet you didn't exercise often in the city—and to keep you from getting bored out of your skull, there was a challenging project conveniently available. Me,'' he told her with some amusement.

She laughed in reaction. ''Well put, Major.''

''But now, babe, it seems to me that you're looking for excuses not to take one of these jobs.'' His voice had become gently chiding. He reached for her hand. ''When you first arrived, you said something that I haven't been able to forget.''

He ran his thumb over her knuckles. ''You said John and I lived on the edge, and you had no intention of living that way. I'm not exactly sure what 'living on the edge' means. We do a dangerous job, but we prepare for it with extreme care. Just as you do.''

Vince paused. He didn't want to voice his suspicions outright. He might suspect the cause of Amanda's grievance against each place she'd visited, but only she could be positive, and he wanted her to reach a conclusion on her own.

He traced a pattern on her palm and continued. "I remember thinking at the time that if you felt that way, your specialization was an odd choice. I can't imagine any job more urgent or critical than being an emergency room doctor. If you wanted peace you should have gone into dermatology."

A.J. laced their fingers together; she was quiet for a long time. Her sandwich lay forgotten on her plate.

Vince didn't even think about rushing her. He would sit here all afternoon if it was necessary.

When she finally spoke, her voice was subdued and held a hint of awe. "I think I get the message. You're saying I needed a vacation, not a change of life-style," she said quietly.

"No. You asked me if you were too hard to please, and I'm saying I don't think so. I'm only presenting you with a possible explanation for why you can't find a satisfactory place. It may not even be the right explanation."

But if it was? Was he suggesting she go back to the city? A.J. shuddered at the thought. But then she wondered whether the shudder was for the demands of the job in the state's largest emergency room or her own state of mind when she'd left there. She'd loved the job when she'd begun at City Hospital. She'd found her duties meaningful and challenging.

Admittedly, she had arrived here exhausted. But her exhaustion had abated very quickly in these bucolic surroundings. "You've made some good points, Vince, and given me a lot to consider. Maybe I was pipe-dreaming when I thought I wanted a simpler life." She glanced at him sideways. "A dermatologist, huh?"

He chuckled under his breath. "Or any other speciality not known for emergencies."

She sighed and picked up her sandwich again. But the bread tasted stale in her mouth. She had to wash it down with milk. "I thought I knew myself pretty well. Maybe I don't."

"I'm not sure any of us does, Tiger. But John is your father. You might have inherited one gene of fondness for living on the edge."

A short time later, while Vince was walking with Dusty around the lake, A.J. finally got a call through to his doctor. Though she was averse to using John's name, she finally did so.

She learned exactly what she'd expected to learn— very little. The man wouldn't be pinned down. "Each case is different," he told her yet again. "Though his vision should return fairly quickly when the cerebral edema—"

"Yes, I understand that," she interrupted. He had a tendency to repeat himself. "By 'quickly,' Doctor, do you mean weeks, days or hours?"

"I need to see him to make a prediction. You should bring him in today." His voice held a note of censure.

"I know, sir, but he refuses to come until next week."

"Convince him," ordered the man. Then he hung up on her.

A.J. held the phone away from her and stared at it. Military doctors were as obnoxious as generals. She repeated the conversation to Vince, but he wouldn't relent.

"Next week," he said firmly.

The next morning Vince awoke alone. He lay still for a moment, his eyes closed. The smell of bacon drifted up from the kitchen below to tempt him.

At last he opened his eyes and stared at the ceiling. There was a dark shape there—an overhead light fixture, he presumed. The contrast was definitely sharper than it had been the day before.

He dressed and headed downstairs. Halfway there he stopped and peered into the room below. The large windows were rectangles of light in the midst of a dark cloud. There was no other definition. He tried not to be either elated or disappointed. Every day could bring improvement. He descended the rest of the way.

"Smells good in here," he said when he entered the kitchen.

"Breakfast is almost ready," said Amanda.

He looked in the direction of her voice but... nothing. Then she moved from the stove, crossed in front of another window, to the sink. He saw the movement! "Amanda?"

A.J. could hear the excitement in his voice. She whirled, dropping the spoon she held. "What?"

"Just now, when you walked from one side of the room to the other, I saw you move in front of the window." His voice was awestruck, as though he couldn't believe the miracle. A grin spread slowly across his face.

"Vince, oh, Vince," she cried. "That's wonderful!" He opened his arms and she went into them to be clasped tightly and warmly against his hard body. Her own vision was suddenly blurred.

She hugged him tight. He lifted her off her feet and turned with her in his arms. He didn't become disoriented—as long as there was a block of light to use as a navigational point he could tell direction. God, thank you! Unbelievable joy filled him. He laughed aloud, exhilarated as never before. "I can see," he rejoiced. "Amanda, I can see!"

He set her down and looked into her face. Or where her face should be. He cupped her cheeks and narrowed his eyes. "But I still can't see your smile," he said, excitement animating his features. "Let's go outside where the light's brighter."

The additional light only made his eyes water. "Damn," he erupted.

"Don't rush it. You'll see everything again, Vince. You will. I'm sure of it. And you'll fly again."

He could hear the thrill in her voice; he knew she was as elated as he was. He smiled, too, and hugged her close. "You wanted me impatient. Now I am. I'm impatient as hell."

The next day Vince's sight was an improvement over the day before. The visual definition was slightly more pronounced. When he finished shaving, which he still did by feel, he leaned close to the mirror and narrowed his eyes as he touched the scar at his temple. In the light over the sink he could see movement, and a dark semicircle where his hair was. His face was still a clouded sphere.

And he still couldn't see Amanda's smile.

"It's begun to snow, Vince," she told him when she came in from walking the dog. "Not a heavy snow, just a dusting. But if the temperature stays below freezing, maybe we'll have enough to build a snowman this afternoon."

His impatience aggravated him, made him uneasy. "What are we going to do until then?"

Amanda interpreted his restlessness correctly. "We're going to clean house," she said with determination.

The cabin didn't require a lot of cleaning. "May arranged for a woman from town to come in twice a month to do whatever had to be done. Since you got here, though, we haven't needed her."

He had begun to realize what a chauvinistic statement he'd made, when Amanda put a dust cloth in his hand. "And just why do you think that is?" she asked sweetly... too sweetly.

He hid a grin. "Housekeeping isn't my calling, Amanda. I don't know how to dust."

"Dusting is a very easy job. You simply wipe all horizontal surfaces. If you don't know how, it's time you learned," she admonished sternly.

"What if I break something?"

"Be careful, and you won't."

He heard her mutter under her breath before the vacuum cleaner drowned out the sound. He had an idea she was denouncing all men who thought housework was beneath them. He laughed under his breath.

Later, she made hot chocolate, and they sat in front of the fire. She read to him from a newsmagazine, a story about an upcoming presidential trip to Europe.

"Is it still snowing?" he interrupted.

"No, it stopped about an hour ago." She picked up the story where she'd broken off.

But before she could finish another sentence, he slapped his knees and got to his feet. "I need to get outside."

She closed the magazine; she wasn't all that interested herself. "That's a good idea. Dusty probably could use a run, too. I'll get our coats."

Dusty was confused and hostile to the snow, growling when he got his feet wet. They laughed at him, and he gave them a pained look. He went to sit on the porch while they built a small snowman. They threw snowballs—Vince grumbled at the unfair advantage she had. "I can't see all that well yet."

The truth was, though, as long as she was moving he could tell where she was. He scored a couple of hits before she figured it out.

When she did, she let loose a piercing war cry and tackled his six-foot-plus body.

Vince was laughing so hard, he almost landed directly on top of her, but he managed to roll to the side at the last second. "I could have killed you, you idiot," he shouted as he hauled her on top of him.

Suddenly, they were both breathless. Her legs were wedged between his. His response was immediate and hard against her thigh. Their lips were only inches apart.

And suddenly he saw her smile.

His heart gave a leap. Her smile was beautiful; it was sexy and sweet; it was seductive. With a soft moan, he reached up and pulled off her knitted cap, releasing the glory of her hair. He threaded his fingers through its thickness and curved his hand around her neck. He dragged her mouth down to his. His tongue painted her lips and plunged inside to taste that beautiful smile.

Amanda's tongue met his eagerly, hungrily. Her senses caught fire from the heat that radiated from him as they lay on the snow-covered ground. In a moment, he had her coat unbuttoned—he was burrowing under her sweatshirt to touch her breasts. "Aman...ah..." He broke off as she moved against his arousal. "I want you. You're so sweet, so soft." His whispered praise became a laughing groan. "And this ground is so hard."

She giggled, a sound quite unlike her. "Well, Major, you do seem to be inspired rather quickly when we're out-of-doors."

"I can be inspired indoors, too, when it's my tiger in my arms," he growled. He kissed and nuzzled her neck. "Let's find a bed."

Amanda's laughter was unsteady. She didn't think he noticed the instinctive, dreamy smile that curved her lips in response to his possessive "my tiger."

"Let's go out to dinner," Amanda said that evening. The day had been very special to her. They had laughed together, and squabbled and made tender, passionate love. And now, for some reason she was unwilling for the day to end.

When the sun went down, her bright mood faded into a shadow. It was an eerie sensation. Oddly, she felt as though today, having been exceptionally happy, was a forecast of impending sorrow.

He raised his head. The wariness in his expression was instantaneous. "Where would we go?"

"There is an inn called Oakleaf on the outskirts of town. The original part of the building is a lovely antebellum redbrick mansion with huge white columns. May says the food is delicious. I've passed it several times and often wanted to stop."

"Amanda, I don't know..."

She gave in without argument. "It's okay. We would probably need a reservation anyway. I'll see what's in the freezer."

"No, wait." He traced the scar at his temple. His hand moved down to stroke his chin thoughtfully. "A strange place, people we don't know—you aren't afraid I'll embarrass you?"

"You could never embarrass me, Vince," she assured him very softly.

"Call the place. See if they can take us."

The man who answered the telephone assured A.J. that the Oakleaf would be delighted to seat them at eight o'clock.

She wore a bright red velvet sheath, a favorite dress that always lifted her spirits, and wondered why she'd been so gloomy before. Vince wore a black blazer and charcoal gray slacks. His tie was the same Christmas red as her dress. He left off the tinted glasses.

The dining room at the inn was well lit, Vince noted with relief, as they followed the maître d' to a table. The man held Amanda's chair and, with a minimum of fumbling, Vince managed to seat himself.

When the waiter presented the menus, Amanda waved him off. "Since we haven't been here before, why don't we have the speciality of the house?" she asked Vince.

"You won't be disappointed," said the waiter. "Our chef is quite good."

Vince nodded. "Fine," he said stiffly. He didn't give a damn what they ate. He wanted to finish and get out of here. Why had he agreed to this?

"May I bring you a cocktail while you wait?" asked the man. He struck a match and lit the single candle in the center of the table.

"I'll have a glass of your house wine," said Amanda.

"I'll have the same," Vince echoed.

She raised her brow at the request. Vince rarely drank. "Scared?" she said when the man left to get their drinks.

"Hell, yes," he answered immediately. "I just realized that I have no idea if I can afford whatever it is I ordered to eat."

She laughed softly. And after a minute he laughed, too.

He laid his hand on the table, palm up, and waited. When she obliged his unspoken request, he curled his fingers warmly around hers. "If I spill soup in my lap, it's on your head, Dr. Upton."

"I'll take that chance, Major. Tonight is our first real date. I've been waiting fourteen years for this, and I intend to enjoy every minute even if we both swim in the soup."

The waiter returned with their wine. Moving his free hand carefully, Vince found the stem of the glass without a slipup. He raised his wine in a toast. "To a beautiful woman. And to many more dates with her."

"Thank you, sir. But it occurs to me that you don't know whether I'm beautiful or not," she teased. She was touched deeply by the promise in his words.

Vince sipped his wine and set the glass down. When he spoke again his voice resonated off her sensitive nerve ends. "I don't have to be able to see you, Amanda, to know that you are beautiful."

Her eyes filled. "Vince—"

"Later, Tiger," he said as the waiter returned with a basket of hot rolls.

When they made love that night, there was a depth of feeling that she had not experienced before. A promise of tomorrow seemed to touch them both, uniting them to each other in a singular bond. The remarkable sensation, a linking of their two souls, was almost spiritual. Again she was tempted to share her feelings, and again she was afraid.

Chapter 10

A.J. fed the dog and gave him fresh water. She was washing her hands in the mudroom when she heard a car. John wasn't expected until tomorrow, which was Saturday; May had been by the cabin earlier this morning and they didn't expect her to come back today.

She stepped outside. When she recognized Ed's car, she tensed. Vince wasn't certain that Ed had anything to do with the fires, but she thought the sheriff should have the opportunity to question him. They had argued about it again yesterday. In her opinion, the coincidental evidence was simply too overwhelming to be ignored.

"Hi, A.J.," Ed called as he got out of the car. He was smiling broadly. "I heard you had some snow up this way yesterday."

She went toward him. "Yes, but it melted during the night. How are you, Ed?" she said, trying to put some warmth into her greeting.

Evidently she had not completely succeeded. He narrowed his eyes and his steps slowed imperceptibly as he joined her. "I talked to John yesterday. He says Vince's memory is coming back. That's great."

"Yes, he's remembered some things." She shrugged, trying to make the recollection seem unimportant. Then she wondered why she felt that was necessary. "Nothing specific, however."

Her father shouldn't have told Ed, she thought suddenly. A cold shiver traveled up her spine.

Then again, why shouldn't John have told Ed? He had no idea of her suspicions. And why did she seem to feel that she had to protect Vince from his best friend? She shook off her misgivings.

He tucked his hands into the pockets of his jacket. "Did Vince tell you my new orders came through? This will probably be the last time I'll get up here."

"Yes, he said you were going to California. I'm sure he'll miss your visits. He told me once that they kept him sane when things got bad." She hesitated, then asked, "Would you like to stay for dinner?"

Vince stood at the back door, squinting hard as he looked out. He could make out the shapes of Ed and Amanda as they talked.

Today his vision was even more definite. Most startling were the colors. He'd forgotten how vivid, how life-giving color was. Amanda had on a red sweater and blue jeans. A red ribbon held the heavy fall of dark hair at her nape.

At this distance, he couldn't make out details, such as their facial expressions, but their body language was easy to read. Amanda was giving Ed her attention yet holding herself slightly aloof, while Ed seemed relaxed, probably unaware that she wasn't perfectly at ease with him.

He was elated to be able to see their shapes, even undefined as they were. He raised his hand to knock on the window, but suddenly his exuberant expression frayed at the edges.

He frowned, struggling against a feeling of doom, a premonition of disaster. All at once, he was rocked by a piercing pain behind his eyes and agony greater than any he'd ever felt. He closed his eyes and staggered away from the door, putting out a hand to the wall to steady himself. He dropped his head.

At last he had his visual. Instead of the figures, he had seen rockets and flames, and pieces of hot shrapnel flying through the air. And smoke billowing up from the ground to envelop the two planes flying side by side. The entire episode in the desert had returned to him in an instant's fireball of knowledge.

He shook his head in a vain attempt to clear it. No, this couldn't be. His memory was playing tricks on him. It had to be wrong.

The pilot who peeled off and attacked the allied tanks was Ed Wilson. Ed had either disobeyed or misunderstood his orders—or he'd gone crazy, had an attack of battle fatigue. Whatever had happened to him had cost lives. American lives.

Ed, his friend, his pal, who had done so much for him, had attacked the tanks and caused his crash.

Vince saw a repeat of the action as though it were rolling across a moving-picture screen. He had seen Ed leave the designated sector. Had followed, had drawn alongside for a visual sighting. And what happened next was the nightmare. Ed, his face distorted, firing his rockets toward the tanks below. Tanks that bore the inverted V of allied forces.

The enemy was quick to take advantage of the attack, and the hole in the allied defenses, coming up out of the sand, moving its own tanks closer, ever closer.

And then the rest of it, the other part that he hadn't been able to remember.

His plane was hit. The rest was a blur, but not because he couldn't see. Everything happened too quickly. Ed's plane disappeared in the smoke from the antiaircraft fire. Vince pulled the ejection switch seconds before his own plane crashed. The concussion from the blast knocked him unconscious.

When he came to, he was on the ground. His shoulder was on fire. His head throbbed agonizingly; he could smell and taste his own blood. It was in his eyes. He tried to wipe his face so he could see.

But he was blinded. He felt the hot desert sands under his feet, and the blazing sun on his head. But the world was as black as midnight.

And he couldn't remember anything beyond the briefing he'd given his squadron, back at the temporary base—before the sortie.

Vince wandered blindly in the desert for almost eighteen hours before a helicopter crew spotted him. All they could tell him was that he was in another sector from where the antiaircraft attack had shot down his plane.

Now fear and rage settled in him. He couldn't make a formal accusation until he got his hands on the crash reports. But he knew in his heart what had happened.

The only thing he didn't know was why. Why the hell had Ed, a well-trained pilot, gone berserk?

Ed had lied to the crash investigators. He had told the investigating body that he had lost sight of Vince during the battle.

He tried to fit this new knowledge into what he'd learned of the fires in the area. Unless Ed was actually insane, Vince couldn't see the battle halfway around the world as a motive for setting a series of forest fires.

Unless all the fires up to now had been decoys. Unless the final plan was to set another fire here at the cabin, to silence him permanently. He was the only witness to the attack on the tanks. Would Ed go that far to cover up his lapse?

Then he had another thought, one that scared him senseless. Amanda had mentioned the smell of gasoline on Ed's clothes. She was the first one to suggest that Ed was here every time a fire was set.

Why the *hell* hadn't he listened to her, talked to the sheriff? It could have been done discreetly. He'd been so damned stubborn, having to have definite proof before he went to the authorities. And now, because of his muleheadedness, she was standing out there with a man who was a murderer. He would call the sheriff, himself. But first he had to get rid of her, get her out of harm's way.

He schooled his expression not to reveal his thoughts and fears and made his way out to join them near the driveway. "Ed? I thought I recognized your voice. When did you get here?"

"A few minutes ago. I came up to celebrate. John says your memory's returning."

Vince felt sick. "Yeah, some of it. Maybe you can help me fill in some blanks. Come on in. I sure am glad you could make it up here one more time before you left," he said, hoping his heartiness didn't sound fake. He schooled himself not to reveal his returning vision. He decided it was wiser to let Ed think he was still totally blind. "I've got a couple of California phone numbers to give you," he said with a suggestive grin as he moved back to the door.

A.J. chuckled.

Vince stopped. "Are you still here, Amanda?" he demanded, his voice deliberately caustic. "I thought you and May had made plans for today."

"Well—"

"Why don't you go now? Ed and I will get along fine without you. Won't we, old buddy?"

Ed didn't answer. His expression was sober and he was watching Vince very closely. She wondered why.

"Take the dog with you," Vince added.

She lifted her chin. "I'll just get my purse," she grated as she passed them on her way into the cabin.

Vince used sarcasm as a weapon, thought A.J. a few minutes later as she turned from the driveway onto the road to town. "A weapon equally as effective as one of those rockets on the planes he flies," she told Dusty, who had climbed eagerly into the passenger seat. His tongue lolled, and he turned to look at her when she spoke again. "He cut me out very neatly—he had to have known his sarcasm would hurt. Unfortunately, Dusty, I reacted in my predictably defensive way." She'd hidden her hurt beneath anger.

He also knew full well that she was going to town for groceries—she'd told him earlier. She and May had no plans, he knew that; yet he'd followed her inside when she went for her purse, suggesting they take in a movie, go to dinner. He'd been very specific. She was to leave the two men alone for the rest of the day and evening. "If he doesn't want me, then I certainly don't want to stay."

Back at the cabin, she'd been too touchy, responding with her heart rather than her head. She hadn't gone very far down the road, however, before her intellect kicked in. "Wait a minute, Dusty." She touched the brake and stared beyond the windshield, thinking hard. "That whole scene was off center."

"Let's go inside," Vince suggested when the sound of Amanda's car had faded away.

"Sure." Ed led the way, removing his jacket when they reached the main room.

"Help yourself if you'd like a drink," Vince said, carefully modulating his voice as he pondered the best way to handle the situation.

Now that he'd gotten rid of Amanda and didn't have to worry about her safety, he felt an urge to simply ram his fist into the other man's face. But he needed to know some things, and he was going to have to keep a strong leash on his temper. He sat at one end of the sofa and stretched his legs out, crossing his ankles and linking his fingers together over his stomach.

Ed had the advantage of clear sight. As he turned toward the bar Vince saw that he had another more deadly advantage, as well—a revolver was wedged under his belt in the small of his back.

But, thought Vince, smiling unpleasantly, Ed didn't know that Vince had an advantage, too. He could see the gun. *And he doesn't know that I'm in as good a shape as I've been in years, thanks to Amanda.*

* * *

Amanda wondered why Vince would choose this particular time to embarrass her in front of Ed. Vince was not insensitive. He could be stubborn and hardheaded, but not spiteful or uncaring. So why, suddenly, had he reverted to sarcasm?

He must have had a damned good reason.

She drummed her fingertips on the steering wheel as she drove, trying to sort out her impression of that conversation. Something was askew—something didn't fit in.

She thought back to another time, when he'd encouraged her to get to know his friend better. Why would he abandon that idea right now and start acting as if he wanted to get rid of her? None of it made sense.

Also, he hadn't said a word to Ed about his improved vision. Ed, his best friend, wasn't privy to this momentous information. That made even less sense.

It was almost as though he was sending her a silent warning. Or was it a message?

Did he want her to do something? Call someone?

Yes, that had to be the answer. Her foot came down hard on the accelerator.

Her thoughts were scrambled, tumbling over each other. She raked her hand through her hair, loosening the ribbon that held it back. She tossed the ribbon aside and struggled to bring order out of the chaos that was her thinking process.

Ed had been in the Middle East with Vince—there was a connection. Something in Vince's returning memory must have indicated a problem. If she hadn't been so damned sensitive, she could have hung around for a while, even if they didn't want her. But no, she had to become defensive and go running off like a silly adolescent.

What could she do? Who could she call for help or advice? She didn't hesitate.

Her father, of course.

Ed poured himself a drink and took one of the wing chairs at right angles to the fireplace. He took a deep swallow and turned to grin at Vince. "You still having trouble with A.J.?"

Vince shrugged. "She's okay." He saw no benefit to be gained by stalling around small talk. "John told you that I'm beginning to get my memory back?"

"Yeah, I'm glad."

"Are you, Ed?" asked Vince quietly.

Ed became very still. "What does that mean?"

"I remember everything. All of it."

Ed set the glass down on the coffee table. He remained bent forward, his spine curved, his elbows resting on his knees. The substance seemed to leak out of him. "I figured it wouldn't be much longer."

Vince stared fixedly at the gun, tempted to grab it, but he was too far away to deal with it in one quick movement. "So you admit it. You want to tell me what sends a top-notch pilot over the edge?"

"Does she know?" Ed asked, jerking his head in the direction of the back door.

Vince remembered just in time that he wasn't supposed to be able to see the gesture. "Amanda? No, she doesn't know anything," he said firmly. "Level with me, Ed. What the hell happened?"

Amanda found a telephone in the parking lot of a strip mall. "Stay here," she said to the dog. Hastily she dug into her billfold for her telephone calling card and dialed John's home number. No answer. She got the number of his office from base information, but there was no answer there, either.

She looked around the small peaceful town, at the shoppers going in and out of the stores, at the drive-in across the way, jammed with the after-school crowd, and tried to tell herself she was being paranoid.

Instead, she grew more worried with every passing minute. She'd been away from the cabin for a quarter hour, but the same dark premonition she'd experienced yesterday descended on her again. A lot could have happened in fifteen minutes. Her anxiety heightened.

Ed had collapsed against the back of the chair. His face sagged, as though his strength was draining from him. "I lost it, Vince. I totally lost it. One minute I was in formation and the next, I was overwhelmed by this sudden, sure sensation that I was about to die. I broke out in a cold sweat, out there in the middle of Hades, the desert. So I ran." He wiped his face with the sleeve of his shirt. His hands were shaking.

Vince could hear the tears in Ed's voice and he had to steel himself not to feel pity. He'd known other pilots who lost their nerve under the tremendous pressure of high-stress combat. With the weapons they carried, and at the speeds they traveled, a second's mistake spelled catastrophe. Not many pilots broke— because they were screened painstakingly—but a few did.

You couldn't doubt yourself; you couldn't let yourself dwell on failure too long or too often. It could result in death—your own or an innocent's. Which was exactly what had happened in this case. Vince felt his anger reassert itself.

Ed went on. "That wasn't the first time I'd broken, either. I lied to the shrinks at my last physical. I've had a couple of blackouts—"

"Why?" demanded Vince, interrupting harshly. "For God's sake, *why* didn't you tell them you were having problems? They would have helped you."

"They would have *grounded* me, damn it."

"Why didn't you tell me?"

"Because you would have grounded me, too. Maybe quicker. I'm exactly like you, Vince. My career is everything to me—my whole life. Surely you, of all people, can understand why I didn't tell them."

His words made Vince pause. Yes, his career was important to him. But his whole life? Everything? Hell, no. He didn't have time to take the thought further.

Ed straightened in his chair. He seemed to be regaining his strength. "And so I screwed up royally."

"You sure as hell did," answered Vince grimly.

A.J. drove back in the direction of the cabin. But instead of turning in when she reached the driveway, she went beyond it, letting the car roll to a stop half on, half off the shoulder. She sat there thinking for a moment. Dusty made a sound of confusion deep in his throat.

Not quite sure why she was doing this, she pulled the car farther off the road, turned off the engine and snapped the dog's leash onto his collar. They got out of the car and she locked it. "I'm probably going to make a fool of myself," she muttered. She could find her way through the woods; she could return to the cabin on foot instead of driving in. And she could see for herself what was going on.

Ed reached for his drink. He took another deep swallow. "I lucked out when you crashed, old buddy. You were the only witness."

Vince took a second to let that sink in. He waited without responding.

"I'm determined, pal, no one will ever know what really happened."

"So it *was* you who set the fires?"

"As distractions," Ed admitted freely. "When a final fire destroys the cabin, the authorities will assume it was started by the same firebug that has been operating here for weeks.

"The fires are my cover. A tragic accident is going to take the life of my best friend. I'll be distraught. You had been through so much. You were on the road to recovery and to be killed in such a peaceful spot as this— I'll mourn the longest. No one will suspect me, a fellow officer who has visited regularly to support his blind friend."

"It's not going to work, Ed," suggested Vince. "We'll end this, man-to-man, right now." He got to his feet.

And Amanda strolled into the room. "Hi."

Vince groaned aloud. "What the devil are you doing back here?" he demanded harshly.

"My car was overheating," she lied. "I had to walk back...." Her words trailed off and her mouth fell open. Vince had moved quickly, trying to get between her and Ed, but Ed was closer. And Ed had pulled a very mean-looking revolver.

"Freeze, Vince! And you, little lady, you'd better keep a tight rein on that leash if you don't want the pooch to die."

Dusty was growling at the man with the gun, jumping, trying to get free. She held on with both hands.

"Put him in the kitchen and close the door," Ed ordered.

This couldn't be happening! She had to drag the frantic dog, but at last she managed to get him through the door. But nothing could drown out his wild barking. Ed was right there when she turned from slamming the door. He grabbed her, twisted her arm behind her back. The revolver was pointed toward her temple. Vince turned white.

Ed smiled at him triumphantly and backed up a dozen feet, dragging Amanda with him. "I *thought* you were pulling my leg. Something about the way you walked out into the yard when I got here tipped me off. You didn't hesitate or take slow cautious steps like you've been taking since the crash. I was sure you could see."

"Ouch, you're hurting my arm, you creep." A.J. struggled angrily against his hold.

It was the wrong thing to say. He yanked her arm higher, until she thought it would break. "Shut up," he screamed, turning the revolver on Vince. "You want to watch me kill him?"

She subsided. "No, oh, God, no."

"Good. I need your help. Go out to my car and bring in the two cans of gasoline you'll find in the trunk." He glanced at his watch. "You have one minute. Then I blow his head off before I come after you."

Desperately her eyes sought Vince's. "Do as he says, Amanda," he told her, raising his voice above the sounds Dusty was making.

She stumbled as Ed released her. She rubbed her arm; it was stiff and sore.

Ed dug in his pocket and tossed her his car keys. "Get going!"

"OhGodohGodohGod," Amanda chanted as she hurried outside. What could she do? What chance did they have? May was going to call the sheriff if she hadn't heard from Amanda in half an hour. Only about fifteen minutes had passed, and it didn't look like postponement was going to be an option with this maniac. She opened the trunk and took out the cans. They were heavy, but she carried them inside.

How much time had passed? "Here they are," she called as she lurched into the room.

The black hole of the revolver was still pointed at Vince's midsection. "Good girl," said Ed. "Now, take the tops off and pour the fuel on the furniture."

"Ed, you can't just—"

"I can do anything I damn well please," said Ed furiously. "Isn't that right, Vince?"

"Do it, Amanda."

"But, Vince—" She was crying.

"Do it!"

Her tears clouded her eyes. She bent to remove the top from the first can. When she tried to lift it her hand slipped. The can fell on its side and the pungent smell of the fuel filled the room as the liquid gurgled onto the floor.

Ed jumped back to keep the fuel from wetting his shoes. "Don't just dump it out like that, you stupid bitch! I want it on the sofa and chairs."

Vince didn't take his eyes off Ed, whose attention was focused on Amanda.

Ed made a threatening gesture, the business end of the gun wavered and Vince took his best chance. He launched his body into the air, and brought Ed down with a flying tackle. "Run, Amanda!" he shouted as he groped for the gun with both hands.

Ed struggled against Vince's grip. He was strong and his finger was still on the trigger.

And at that moment, fifty pounds of angry dog launched itself up over the kitchen sink and into the pass-through opening. His nails scrabbled on the slick counter while he took a quick inventory. He barely paused before he leapt to the floor and raced to Vince's aid.

Cursing viciously, Ed rolled to the side and got off one shot before the dog's teeth sank into his wrist. He screamed.

The bullet sailed over Vince's head, but punctured the second can of gasoline. Ed dropped the gun and screamed again. "Get him off me!"

Vince landed a blow to Ed's jaw and the man collapsed, just as the gasoline exploded. The blast knocked Amanda off her feet.

"Tiger!" Vince yelled frantically. "Tiger!"

"I'm all right," she shouted back.

Dusty went to her side.

The room was filling quickly with smoke and flames. Vince dragged himself to his knees and then to his feet. He kept his head low. Stumbling, he made his way to her side and went down on one knee beside her. He yanked her into his arms. "Babe, are you okay? Are you really okay?" His hands shook severely as he ran them over her legs, her arms, her face, to see for himself that she wasn't badly hurt. Aside from a few bruises and scratches she seemed to be uninjured.

She was crying, too, and trying to hold him. "I'm singed but okay. What about you?"

"I'm alive." He wrapped her in his arms. "God, when I saw that bastard point that gun at you, I wanted to kill him."

The heat was growing more intense. Dusty whined and Vince saw the flames begin to lick at the banister. He helped Amanda to her feet. "Let's get out of here," he shouted.

"Wait, Vince. We can't leave Ed. We have to get him out."

Vince ground his back teeth together. Left to himself, he wasn't certain what he would have done. But his tiger would never leave a human being to die, no matter what his sins.

"You take Dusty and go outside," he told her.

When she would have protested, he whirled on her. "Don't argue with me, Amanda. I'll bring him."

The sirens were audible in the distance when he reached the back door, staggering under Ed's deadweight. Amanda ran forward to help him drag Ed away from the fire.

They both collapsed on the grass as the sirens drew nearer. Dusty stood guard over Ed's prone body.

Suddenly the small grassy area of the yard was filled with people. May, the sheriff, deputies, firemen and hoses, forest rangers, all milled about while an ambulance made its way up the drive.

Amanda tried to stand up, to assure May that she was all right. But suddenly her knees gave way. She heard Vince cry out as she fell, and then she knew nothing else.

Chapter 11

May drove Vince to the hospital in Amanda's car. All the way into town, he held a wrinkled bit of red ribbon in his fist and prayed. When they reached the emergency room, they had been reassured by one of the doctors that Amanda was going to be fine, but no, Major Thornborough couldn't see her tonight.

Then the doctor looked more closely at his blackened clothes and red, burning face. "Aren't you the major who's been recuperating at the Upton cabin? Come in here. I want to check you over."

The smell of the hospital was smothering, medicinal. A short while later, over his protests, Vince was wheeled away.

"Just overnight, Major Thornborough," said the nurse who pushed him briskly along the corridors to a room. "The doctor wants to make sure there are no aftereffects from smoke inhalation." An aide presented him with a plastic bag of amenities and told him how to adjust the temperature, while another nurse appeared to take his vital signs.

Without complaint, he waited for them to finish. He'd decided that was easier than arguing with them. Doctors! They never really listened.

He smiled to himself. Even Amanda. If she decided something—like an exercise program—was in the best interest of a patient, she would keep the pressure on until the patient capitulated.

At last they left him alone. He had to get out of this bed. He'd be damned if he was going to take anybody else's word that she was all right. He had to make certain for himself. He found his soot-smeared jeans and shirt and put them on.

He must have looked like hell. But the halls were almost deserted at this time of night. And, thank God, the volunteer on duty in the lobby had gone home. He thumbed through the papers on the desk. He made his way to the opposite wing and found Room 202.

When Vince entered, John was sitting beside Amanda's bed, holding on to her hand as though he couldn't let go.

"I didn't know you were here, John. Where is May?"

The older man raised tear-reddened eyes to his. "I sent her home."

Vince nodded, but he had eyes only for Amanda. He crossed to the opposite side of the bed and took her other hand in his. Her palm was dry and warm.

He looked down at her, reveling in her safety as well as the luxury of his restored sight. Her personality was so filled with character and determination that, without his vision, he found it easy to forget how small she was. But looking down at her now, he was reminded of a doll that had been dragged through a chimney.

Her eyebrows were singed, as was her hair—someone had trimmed off the burnt ends, and it was a great deal shorter. Soft curls framed her face.

He blinked hard. Her cheeks and forehead had been smeared with the same ointment that was on his. A small tube fed oxygen into her nostrils. He could look at her forever and never get tired of the beautiful vision she presented.

God, he loved her. He closed his eyes and shook his head. He'd never had the guts to tell her so. Every time the urge hit him, he'd come up with crazy excuses. Well, no more.

John indicated with a jerk of his head that he wanted to talk in the hall. "How are you feeling, son?" he said when the door closed behind them. He sounded rusty, as though he hadn't spoken for a long time. "You should be in bed yourself."

"I'm fine," Vince said, dismissing his burns. Though they were red, none of them was serious. "Has she regained consciousness?"

"Once, in the emergency room. The doctor gave her an injection, but not before she made him report on your condition. She told me then that your vision had returned. But I knew already."

Vince ignored the last. "Did she tell you what happened? Did she tell you the bastard held a gun on her?" He felt his anger return and shuddered when he recalled her slight body in Ed's grasp, the pistol at her temple.

John nodded and clasped the younger man's shoulder. "And on you. I have to say, I would never have suspected him of setting those fires."

"Amanda suspected him because of the timing. She figured out that his visits always coincided with the fires, but I wouldn't let her go to the sheriff with the story."

"For God's sake, why not?" John demanded, an angry frown forming across his brow.

Vince hesitated, then looked away from John. "I had some holier-than-thou hang-up about accusing someone without firm evidence." A heartbeat of silence elapsed. Neither man seemed to know what to say. "It's my fault she was drawn into this."

John looked away, too. "Don't blame yourself," he said after a minute. "Did Ed ever tell you why he set the fires?"

"The fires were incidental. Let's find a seat somewhere, and I'll tell you the whole story." He asked the nurse at the desk where they could find a cup of coffee.

"I'll give you coffee from our staff lounge, but you really need to be in bed, Major."

"News travels fast," he said, grinning. He followed her into the room behind the desk, and accepted two cups of coffee.

"This is a small hospital," she answered. "I should call your floor nurse."

"I have to report to the general. Then I'll go back to my room," he lied. But he gave himself away when he looked toward Amanda's room and asked, "Will you call us if Dr. Upton wakes?"

The nurse followed his gaze. "You could sit there all night. She isn't going to wake until morning. Look, I won't say anything, but take it easy, will you?"

"Thanks." He joined John, and they took their coffee and moved into a nearby waiting room.

For the next half hour John absorbed the tale, visibly shaken and horrified when Vince told him about the attack on allied tanks. "The Pentagon is investigating that attack. I'll have to get this information to them immediately. Ed will probably never face a court-martial, of course. From your report, I gather he's a deeply disturbed man."

"What about his physical condition?" The subject left a bad taste in his mouth, but he had to ask.

"The hospital made arrangements to fly him to Atlanta. He was burned pretty badly."

Vince surged to his feet and began to pace. "The bastard. I would have left him there. Amanda insisted I drag him out."

"No, son, you wouldn't have left him," John stated soberly.

"He tried to kill her."

"He tried to kill both of you. Thank God, he didn't succeed." John rubbed exhaustedly at his face.

Vince pulled up; he returned to his chair and sank down into it. He looked at his friend for a moment and had a thought. "How did you get here so fast, John? I thought you were coming tomorrow."

John Upton's face turned a blazing, flaming red. He cleared his throat. "Well, uh, actually—I came up a day early."

When Vince gave him a quizzical look, he went on. "To stay with May."

"To spend the night with her, you mean?" Vince didn't think John's face could be any more red, but he was wrong.

The older man made an effort to reassert himself. He straightened in his chair. "Yes. But it's all very aboveboard. We are going to marry," he stated formally.

"Good, I'd hate to have to come after you with a shotgun."

It took John a full minute to realize Vince was joking.

The morning brought the sheriff with dozens of questions. Vince showered, and donned his filthy clothes—the only clothes he had, as a matter of fact. He answered the questions, but he ignored the breakfast tray. He urgently wanted to be with Amanda.

But when he arrived at her door, it was almost a replay of last night. John still sat beside her bed. Amanda was still asleep.

"Is she all right?" he whispered, worried. "Shouldn't she be awake?"

"The doctor says to let her sleep as long as she will," John answered in an equally soft whisper.

Vince took up the vigil in a chair across the bed from John.

They sat quietly for a few minutes. Then John broke the silence. "Have you called your doctor to tell him that you can see again?"

Vince waited a minute before answering. "Not yet. Amanda talked to him a few days ago, when I noticed the first sign of improvement, but..." He inhaled deeply. This wasn't going to be an easy subject to discuss with John.

Ed Wilson had argued with the zeal of a fanatic that, like Vince, his career was his life. That he had expected Vince to understand was a damned insult. Vince's commitment to the air force was strong—he would always love flying—but from that moment he had known that, for himself at least, the military was no longer paramount in his life.

"I don't know what I'm going to do about the air force," he said to John. "I'm in love with Amanda. I want to marry her. I don't know how she feels," he said, weariness evident in his voice even though they continued their conversation in whispers. "I do know she hates the military with a vengeance. But that might work out."

"What do you mean? You'd quit?" John was appalled, as Vince had known he would be.

"It may not be my choice. My sight has returned, John, but it's not perfect."

"Give it time."

"I have a feeling I may never be jet-worthy again. And I sure as hell don't want to sit at a desk."

John stared at him. At last the older man sighed.

"Things will work out. Don't do anything rash."

"Damn it, John," he whispered fiercely. "Don't give me platitudes. I'm not going to sit around waiting for fate to decide my future. There are a lot of things I can do that will make me happy and keep me in aviation. I can start a small flying school, or a freight service. Or maybe get consultant work with the aircraft plant in Marietta. I have a degree in aeronautical engineering. I could design. Whatever I do, I'm going to do it wherever Amanda lives. If she'll have me, she's worth it."

"Oh, she'll have you, all right," said Amanda, hoarsely from the bed. Both men were instantly on their feet.

She smiled at her father. "Would you raise the head of my bed, please?"

"Wait, babe," said Vince, his hand on her shoulder.

"Please raise the bed," she said firmly. "The two of you have been talking over me for the past five minutes. I want to be upright for the rest of this."

Vince leaned over her, his long arms straight, fists on the bed beside her shoulders. A smile spread across his face. "You do, huh? I don't know, I kind of like you this way—flat on your back and sort of helpless."

"In your dreams, ace." She raised her arms and pulled him down to her. Their lips met, melded in a sweet kiss of promise.

John cleared his throat, found the apparatus and pushed the button to elevate his daughter's head. The action recalled both of them to the present.

A.J. reluctantly dropped her arms and turned to her father. "I tried to call you yesterday, John. When I believed there was trouble, you were the first person I thought of turning to for help."

A look of dawning pleasure lightened John's weary features. "You did?" he asked.

She reached for his hand and grasped it firmly. "Yes. We haven't made much effort in the past to understand each other. I think we should spend some time together."

"I'd like that, Amanda," he said, covering her fingers with his hand. "I would really like that."

A.J. thought she saw moisture in her father's eyes. *Nonsense,* she told herself. *The general, crying? Not a chance.*

He patted her hand. "I have news for you two. I'll be back in a minute," he said.

He left the room. Vince looked at Amanda and shrugged, then he smiled tenderly. "That was a nice thing you did, babe."

"It was long overdue." Without breaking eye contact, she patted the bed. "Sit here beside me. I have so many questions. Where's Dusty? We have to get him a very large steak."

"May took him home with her." He sat and drew her under his arm, her shoulder against his chest. He picked up her free hand in his and looked down. Her knuckles were scraped so when he lifted them to his lips, he did so very gently. But he had no intention of waiting another minute to pose this most important question. "Tiger, I love you. I hope to have the rest of our lives to answer all your questions. If I resign from the air force, will you marry me?" he asked softly but earnestly.

Amanda tilted her head back and looked up at him. She realized from his expression how deeply his feelings went. Her answer was vital to him, as vital as he was to her life, her happiness. A smile dawned like the sun on her face as she laid her hand against his cheek. Her eyes filled and she gave a short, choked laugh. "I love you, Vince. I'll marry you, and you *will* stay in the air force."

He gathered her close. "No, babe. I wouldn't do that to you."

"Vince, I'm a doctor. I can practice in almost any emergency room in the world and be happy. Especially since you pointed out to me that I might not like small-town life after all. The air force is what you do— I wouldn't dream of taking you away from the life you love."

"Even if I have a choice—which I may not have if my vision isn't better than normal—I can do other things," he persisted stubbornly. "I'm getting out."

She prickled. "But, Vince—"

"I think the two of you have time to argue over this later," said John from the doorway. "Right now, I have an announcement to make." He stepped aside, and May came into the room. John took her hand. "May has consented to be my wife."

There were hugs and kisses and congratulations all around. A.J. and Vince exchanged a warm, knowing smile. She was delighted to see her father acting like soft putty in May's hand, and Vince knew it.

May informed A.J. and Vince that she had rooms prepared for them at her house. "And—" she held up a shopping bag "—I brought both of you jeans and shirts. It isn't much, but at least you'll have a change of clothes until you can shop for yourselves."

"Thank you, May," said Amanda. She squeezed Vince's hand. "We'd love to stay with you, but we'll only need one room."

John inhaled and tucked his chin into his collar as he looked down at his daughter. He opened his mouth to say something.

Vince cleared his throat and looked straight at John, daring him to protest. He had no intention of letting Amanda out of his sight for a long, long time. He wanted to lie with her, to hold her close to his heart, and he knew she felt the same way. They would have the marriage certificate, but he was not going to wait for it.

A hint of a smile crossed his face. Maybe it was dirty pool, but he wasn't above reminding John that he had sneaked into town a day before he was supposed to arrive, even if it embarrassed May.

The men broke off the glances. "I suppose that's all right," John said finally.

"It will only be until Monday," A.J. said. She had caught the tension in the air but had no idea of the reason for it. "Vince has to check in with his doctors in Atlanta. I'm sure he'll have to have many tests. Darn, I wish I hadn't given up my apartment. Well, we'll find a place and—"

Her words were cut off when Vince covered her mouth with his. "As John says, we'll talk about this later," he commented when he lifted his head. His voice had taken on the familiar tone of command she often heard in her father's.

"May, I'm so glad you're going to be my stepmother," said A.J. a short time later. The men had left them alone, and May had helped her dress. She was still a bit stiff as she linked her arm in the older woman's.

They walked out of the hospital, into the autumn sunshine. The men waited by the car at the curb. "We'll have great times. Do you play tennis?"

"My God, I hope not!" said the general.

* * * * *

HE'S AN

AMERICAN HERO

A cop, a fire fighter or even just a fearless drifter who gets the job done when ordinary men have given up. And you'll find one American Hero every month only in Intimate Moments—created by some of your favorite authors. This summer, Silhouette has lined up some of the hottest American heroes you'll ever find:

July: HELL ON WHEELS by Naomi Horton—Truck driver Shay McKittrick heads down a long, bumpy road when he discovers a scared stowaway in his rig....

August: DRAGONSLAYER by Emilie Richards—In a dangerous part of town, a man finds himself fighting a street gang—and his feelings for a beautiful woman....

September: ONE LAST CHANCE by Justine Davis—A tough-as-nails cop walks a fine line between devotion to duty and devotion to the only woman who could heal his broken heart....

AMERICAN HEROES: Men who give all they've got for their country, their work—the women they love.

IMHER05

Take 4 bestselling love stories FREE

Plus get a FREE surprise gift!

Silhouette Books has done it again!

Opening night in October has never been as exciting! Come watch as the curtain rises and romance flourishes when the stars of tomorrow make their debuts today!

Revel in Jodi O'Donnell's STILL SWEET ON HIM—
Silhouette Romance #969
...as Callie Farrell's renovation of the family homestead leads her straight into the arms of teenage crush Drew Barnett!

Tingle with Carol Devine's BEAUTY AND THE BEASTMASTER—
Silhouette Desire #816
...as legal eagle Amanda Tarkington is carried off by wrestler Bram Masterson!

Thrill to Elyn Day's A BED OF ROSES—
Silhouette Special Edition #846
...as Dana Whitaker's body and soul are healed by sexy physical therapist Michael Gordon!

Believe when Kylie Brant's McLAIN'S LAW—
Silhouette Intimate Moments #528
...takes you into detective Connor McLain's life as he falls for psychic—and suspect—Michele Easton!

Catch the classics of tomorrow—*premiering* today—
only from ♥ *Silhouette*

Relive the romance...
Harlequin and Silhouette
are proud to present

by Request

A program of collections of three complete novels by the most requested authors with the most requested themes. Be sure to look for one volume each month with three complete novels by top name authors.

In June: **NINE MONTHS** Penny Jordan
Stella Cameron
Janice Kaiser

Three women pregnant and alone. But a lot can happen in nine months!

In July: **DADDY'S HOME** Kristin James
Naomi Horton
Mary Lynn Baxter

Daddy's Home... and his presence is long overdue!

In August: **FORGOTTEN PAST** Barbara Kaye
Pamela Browning
Nancy Martin

Do you dare to create a future if you've forgotten the past?

Available at your favorite retail outlet.

REQ-G

Silhouette Books
is proud to present
our best authors,
their best books...
and the best in
<u>your reading pleasure!</u>

Throughout 1993, look for exciting
books by these top names in
contemporary romance:

DIANA PALMER—
Fire and Ice in June

ELIZABETH LOWELL—
Fever in July

CATHERINE COULTER—
Afterglow in August

LINDA HOWARD—
Come Lie With Me in September

When it comes to passion,
we wrote the book.

BOBT2